A Dram of Fresh Water

BECKY JAMES

BECKY TAMA

CLARKENHOME PRESS

Also by Becky James

DARK TIDES

Co-authored with Becky Tama

A Dram of Freshwater

The Shadow of Death

The Thief of Souls

THE KING'S SWORDSMAN

Upper Young Adult / New adult sword and sorcery.

The Tenets in the Tattoos

The Bind of Blood and Bonds

The Limit of the Lonely Man

The Tempered Turns of Time

The Mettle of the MasterMage

For news from the author, check out www.beckyjamesauthor.co.uk

Paperback ISBN: 978-1-9168774-4-3

Book cover design: Allegra Pescatore

Clarkenhome Press

Gloucestershire

GL2 5DR

www.clarkenhomepress.com

To my wonderful beta reader Kristen Braddock, thank you so much for your wisdom, insight and the little comments going "!!!!!!!"
I treasure them all.

To my fantasy beta reader and ongoing supporter Michelle Menezes, thank you for your thoughts and Dram is all the better for your comments!
I hope you can find it in you to forgive him ;)

And Wren – I believe in you <3

Thank you to everyone who suggested the chocolate goodies! (Check out the note at the back for more!)

The
Fae Realm
Beyond
the Veil

CHAPTER 1
Darla

Taking a deep breath, Darla flung her shoulders back and raised her new arms to the sky. The sky! Even that was incredible. She had seen it before, of course, but today was different. *Everything is different when viewed with new eyes.*

She sat on the grainy sands of the shore, and beyond that was a long, flat bed. *Ground, they call it here.* Or perhaps it was grass, soil, coast, shore, beach, field, farm, land, so many words beyond her feeble few. Sand and silt she knew all too well, suspended in the waters surrounding her, but out here on the shore, the air was clear. It felt uncomfortable, yes, but stretching one's boundaries always did.

Darla flexed her uncovered fins—*hands*—and straightened her sore legs. Her knees knocked together, a surge like a wave in her stomach at the long limbs which would help her stand upright rather than lolling flat.

The horizon lay clear and clean for miles around. No more clouded vision, visibility less than a flipper in front of her nose. No more sifting through the water, forced to taste her way around the sea. She could use her eyes, and, oh, what her new human eyes could see.

"Neri! Come see this!"

Her sister Neri snorted from the sea, the silver seal reluctant to beach.

"Come on!" As Darla shouted, strands played over her lips. She ripped them out of her way, her head hurting, and she held hanks of long hair in her hands. Hair, rather than her fur.

Thinking of fur made her cast about for her sealskin. It lay discarded, a brown husk pulsing with an unsteady light. She could not touch it; she would be instantly transformed back into a seal, and the chance to explore the human world would be wasted for seven long years until she could return again.

Neri snorted again, distressed.

Darla rolled her eyes. "I won't tell you again. This is our only opportunity."

With great reluctance, Neri hauled herself onto the seashore, and Darla watched her sister's transformation. Selkies shed their sealskins once every seven years, and then only for seven days, but the females of the colony were reticent to talk about their own visits. Dire stories of the follies of staying for longer than a human week had filled the sister's ears ever since they were pups, but vague promises of dire outcomes just induced undirected anxiety. Darla would be as careful as she knew how with her personal safety and of course never speak of being a selkie if that was the matriarch's wish, but she was determined to spend a week in the light, even if it was just once. At her twenty-five winters, she was more than capable of handling herself and keeping one little secret, no matter what lay beyond the sandy horizon.

Her sister's fur, a sylph-like silver, reflected the sun. Darla shaded her eyes; the light was bright up here, but she could still see perfectly. Neri's fur stuck up in places, looking brittle and stick-like, and then it dried all of a sudden, as if a hot wind had scoured across her. Neri yelped as her skin sloughed off and Darla held onto her sobbing sister's shoulders as she shook.

"I don't like it, Darla! I want to go back!" Neri curled her fists into Darla's hair. Her little sister squinted in the sunlight, then shrieked and buried her face against Darla's chest. "You don't look like you!"

Darla smoothed a hand over her sister's shoulders. "But I am me," she cooed, keeping her voice calm and level. Her heart beat with insistent urgency, reminding her of the time she had left with none to waste. She needed to go and explore the land, the mountains, the forests and find the edge of the sky, so blue and far away and calling to her endlessly... but Neri needed her. "I am here, little one."

Sniffing, Neri collected herself, and Darla held her out at arm's length. "Why, you're beautiful!"

Neri's white hair swept down to her ankles, her long, pale limbs stick-like. She had a small nose now, which twitched as she tried to take in the new scents of the shoreline. Her deep brown eyes were still filled with sadness; even confronting this exciting adventure with a new form, Neri looked bereft.

Darla caught a handful of her own hair again as it flapped in the wind. Dark, the colour of Dover sole, curling and twisting around her hands as if to ensnare them. *I wonder what I look like?* As a seal, Darla had been brown and silver, stripes of both rippling along her sides to confound predators, a flashing blur of sunlight and shadow when she swam.

"This is horrible." Neri slumped. Then she shrieked, pushing out of Darla's arms. Neri's silver sealskin rolled along the shore, snatched by the waves and dragged across the shingle. Neri fumbled after it, her human limbs flailing and gawky, and Darla hid a chuckle behind her hand.

Thigh deep in water, Neri snatched up her skin, clutching it to her breast. The skin embraced her back, two halves becoming whole, and Neri sank back under the waves, a silver seal once more.

"Neri!" Darla's mouth fell open. "Now you cannot change back for a full seven years!"

When Neri resurfaced with a spray of water, it was with a defiant glare in her black seal eyes.

"Oh, darling Neri". Darla put her chin in her hand. *"If only you would use that defiance against what we've been taught and told, not against me."* The beat of the sea against the shore matched her heartbeat, pounding with purpose. The racing waves tried again and again to clasp the land, only to fall back and drain away, defeated, but never dissuaded for long. It matched the longing inside her. *I want to see it. I want to touch it. I want to hold it.* It would be a shame if she let this opportunity slip through her fingers, just as water trickled back along grooves of sand. "I want to see what it's like up here," she whispered to herself.

Darla stood. "Well, I shall not waste this." Dusting her hands, sand scraped her palms. Unknowns awaited her, new sights and sounds, but also other sensations. What would awaken her senses, what memories would she bring back to the colony for them to share?

Neri barked something at her, but Darla couldn't understand her in this form. In a way, she had never understood her sister's need to cling to the familiar.

Darla welcomed change. Darla wanted to be changed by it.

CHAPTER 2

Rory

Rory wished he could change. *This outfit is riding up my ass.* But, if he'd say so himself, it was a nice ass.

He had been summoned to his sister Orla's side. It really was Queen Orla now; she never let Rory or their brother Kade forget it. She had sent a servant who'd instructed him to arrive at the throne room itself, and who then proceeded to dictate what he should wear. Rory had pretended to take all the instructions in—white shirts, tails, tie—smiling and nodding, but when the hassled fae faded away, he leaned back in his chair and threw his feet up onto the table. If he had been in cat form, his tail would have been twitching side to side; as it was, his fingers drummed on the back of his hand. It was hard work, constantly annoying Orla.

Their mother had insisted on perfect obedience. When she died, Orla seemed keen on inheriting her iron will and ruthless streak along with the throne. Kade was too much of a dreamer to take anything seriously. He believed in the good within everyone, a perspective that Rory both loathed and loved and had no desire to rip away from his brother.

At five minutes after the appointed time, he stretched and

got to his feet, pulling on his leather jacket. He made sure his daggers were securely in their holsters, small, serrated edges honed and ready to be pulled out at a moment's notice. After shoving his feet into his well-worn boots, he sauntered toward the throne room, smiling and nodding at all the fae bustling around pretending to be busy in the tumbledown castle the Cat Sidhe called home this season.

Ten minutes after the message said Orla would be expecting his arrival, Rory banged open the doors to the throne room. "So sorry I'm late, sister dear!"

The throne was magnificent, a study in intimidation. Bones of beasts had been exhumed and artfully placed, held together by a mass of metal. Hanging over it was a pelt of indeterminate origin, brown and bristly, so thin it appeared brittle and liable to tear at any moment, but Rory knew it was soft to the touch, and strong. He had tried to tear it once, in a fit of pique at Orla, and gotten nowhere, even with his claws. The thing had belonged to their mother, and Orla kept it on the throne for sentimental reasons, as if Mother would be back any moment to put it over her shoulders.

The throne loomed on the dais, awaiting grovelling petitioners or snivelling supplicants or some other poor wretches, but it was utterly empty. Rory hesitated.

"Ah, there you are, Ruairí." Orla—or Órlaith, if she was insisting on full names—came in from the main doors to the throne room, behind Rory. She was taller than Rory and shared his flaming red hair, wearing hers loose today to waft and billow down to her knees. She smiled at his attire. "Good. You're perfectly ready to go hunting for me, I see."

Rory seethed. He had been tricked into doing exactly as Orla expected him to do. Tipping his head back, he leaned against the doorframe. "Dressed for it, perhaps. Willing and motivated? Not likely."

Orla's full red lips parted. "Many are the men around court

who would leap at my command. I find it interesting that my brother needs a different type of inducement."

Rory shrugged. "There must be some upsides to being a prince of the court, no?" Turning, he made his way further into the throne room, and Orla followed, high heels clicking on the polished obsidian.

The tall arches yawned over him, the crumbling ceilings harbouring shadows. The tattered remains of the stained glass windows threw stark images on the floor, depicting the World-heart river travelling across all four of the elements that made up the fae realm. Air, up in the mountains, where the World-heart was a multitude of little bubbling streams. Fire, full of frothy waterfalls. Water, where the Worldheart turned fat and sluggish as it joined together, and finally the elemental domain of Earth, where the Worldheart careened off the edge of the known world and into the Otherworld. It all looked so cheery and bright, even with the chipped and missing panes, but the reality? Not so much.

Rory halted, feet at the edge of the depiction of the World-heart river, which was a kind of bluish silver, a light somehow purer than white. The Worldheart that passed by this stolen castle was deep underground, accessible only by a strange organism the Cat Sidhe had found, and it rewarded being fed with souls with small beads of concentrated magic. Magic the Cat Sidhe badly needed.

Orla stopped next to the picture of a Cat Sidhe. The stealer of souls, slinking about in the dark and snatching spirits, black cats with white spots dancing around bodies laid out to rest. Black was not the Cat Sidhe's only colour; Rory himself was red. Gathering what they could, the Cat Sidhe would take the souls here, to encourage the soul to add their essence to the world, to re-enter as pure energy.

"Ruairí." Orla's voice was soft.

That she either felt or pretended to feel sorry for him was

beside the point; they had no choice. He wiped his face, muttering, "I wish you wouldn't call me that."

She laid a hand on his back. "You cannot fathom how sorry I am to place this burden on you and our brother."

Rory moved, dipping his shoulder so her hand slid off him. "Leave Kade out of it. He's distracted anyway."

Orla's gaze studied his, a searching gaze only an older sister could possess, and not tempered by time. Then she handed him refined magic, concentrated into small hard ovals like marbles. "This is all I can spare for now, so do return with a bountiful supply."

He put them into his pocket with the others, weighing them in his hand. A paltry amount, barely enough for a journey there and back or a few glamours if he used them to charge his garnet.

Orla tucked her hair behind her ear. "I'm close to getting at Shay, I think," she murmured, "but we do need more magic, Rory."

Rory clasped his hands behind his back. It was always the same need, the same dragging want, the unfillable hole. While the Cu Sidhe reigned and took the souls of men and women, fae and fairy, human and humdrum out of the equation, magic failed to be replenished. The small offerings he could scavenge and scrounge were but trifles, a cat bringing in a dead mouse when there were a thousand mouths to feed. And all for what? For the world not to end?

At least it would be over, if it all ended. Rory pushed that thought away in case it showed on his face.

Circling him, Orla let out a low, slow breath. "It will be dangerous. While you're out in the human realm to hunt, my sight is limited."

"I won't get into a confrontation with Shay, then." Rory flexed his hands. "Never fear, sister. I will either return or die in the attempt." *And the thought that I might die... How excellent.*

Orla's long, languid steps took her to the throne. As she sat, she drew the bristly fur onto her lap, fingertip stroking the very edge. "Go, then, and good hunting."

With a jaunty salute, Rory left the throne room. *Oh, gods. The human realm again.* Another long, cold trip ahead of him. But still, death could wait at the end of it, and that put a spring in Rory's step.

He made his way toward the one Veil portal in the Cat Sidhe's environs. There, the fabric of reality had been torn and somehow propped open, leaving a hovering portal, half as tall as he currently stood, a foot from the ground. Only the Cat Sidhe could rip the Veil, but it took substantial amounts of magic and feeding it parts of your own life essence, and Rory was poor at that. Instead, Rory would use one that had stood for generations. As for why it was still open instead of self-healing like all the others, Rory had no idea, but they used it anyway.

Guards nodded at him and retreated, watching with some curiosity. Orla had the portals guarded for her people's safety as much as anything else. Portal travel was hard on a fae, and it wasn't as if there was spare magic lying around to replenish oneself with. Reaching toward the ground, Rory shifted into his cat form, the transition smooth as he absorbed his clothes. He walked into the portal as nonchalantly as he could, twitches pricking up his spine. Despite lack of air in this between-place, a current ruffled his fur, his paws hot against the floor. *Is this what oblivion is like?*

Trotting down the portal Rory stretched his soul senses along, half concentrating on his surroundings, half immersed in feeling. Rory stilled when echoes of pain danced along the edges of his awareness. *A large collection of souls.* Yes, this was a huge haul. An accident, perhaps? That could account for a series of lives lost one after another like this, collecting together.

Rory flailed at the side of the Veil, intense pressure pushing back on his limbs. He could make a tear through this old portal, yes, if he fuelled it with his life energy, and he wasn't sure how much of that he had. Some days, it took everything in him to get out of bed; some days, he didn't even make it that far.

I could die doing this.

Squaring up to where he felt the souls pulsing, rich and bursting with energy, just beyond the Veil, he steeled himself. He needed to be fast; if the Cu Sidhe did not know about the accident, they soon would, and he didn't fancy facing off against the dogs.

He set his jaw. He didn't need to use any raw magic for this, using his ability as a Cat Sidhe. He began peeling apart the layers of reality like hunting through a tower of laundry to get to the time and the place where these souls languished. There were so many, they would power the realm for a significant period of time. His paws ached as if he held on by the tips of his claws, but he pushed through the pain.

Once the tear was made, he shifted his paws into fingers, the better to grasp and force apart. He strained, muscles heaving and then burning with effort. *It isn't working.* He pressed hard, forcing his own life energy into the tear to make the connection hold fast. His fingers hurt as if they burned to the core but without heat. *Damn it!* He shoved, and at last his hand slipped into the human realm with a bite of pain like a steel trap springing shut around his wrist. Rory pulled back, but his energy was too entangled with the tear. He fell, unable to stop, fingers clawing out to grasp something, anything, before darkness closed over his head.

CHAPTER 3
Darla

Slipping her finger through the sand, Darla catalogued each new sensation. Grit grinding against flippers was one thing, but now she had extra independent appendages. Each one sent new signals, and she closed her eyes, the better to dwell on them. Pain, yes, a small scratching from each grain of sand, but each of her new mini-limbs—fingers—moved in a different direction. Like a shoal, they could move in concert, or they could wiggle in sequence as a ripple.

The air had currents of its own, the wind, which she could feel even in this form. *How far up do these air currents go?* She tilted her head back, trying to focus on what sky she could see between the blooms of clouds, scudding like sediment across the horizon. How many layers were there of seabed, sediment, water column, land, clouds, and air column? When did it end, and what was next, high above?

Having two separate appendages instead of her tail was easier to get used to than she had thought. Some ancestral memory of being on land must have awoken the sensation in her, for she found her strong tail muscles served her well even separated like this, and balance was something she used every day in the sea.

Another distressed blow of water came from Neri. Darla smiled sweetly at her sister. "I will see you back here in seven sleeps," she promised, and she headed toward where scrubs of green and grey met the tan of the sands, the strands bending in the brisk air currents, but then she stopped as cold slipped over her human skin..

Behind her, slumped in the sand, lay her seal pelt, throbbing in her awareness. Limp and lifeless, it called to her. She couldn't leave it there exposed on the bay to predators, but neither could she touch it; she would be instantly transformed back as Neri had been.

Darla hunted for some tools, gathering two thick, long sticks, scoured to smoothness by the pounding waves and bleached white by the sun. Tree limbs, Darla knew, though she had yet to see an actual tree. What colour had these things been originally, before the sea had stripped and marred them into these ghostly hues?

They were perfect for her purpose, and she used them in tandem to pick up her skin. It snagged and slipped, still slippery even though it was drying, her brown fur sticking up in all directions. Touching it sent a phantom poke on her back and shoulder, something digging in. She bit her lip and bore it.

She manoeuvred her skin to where a set of three buried stones formed a loose sentry post. Her fingers were quite weak unless she pressed them together to make a paddle, and she dug a hole as deep as the length of her new arm. She prodded the skin and it slipped in. The idea of covering it made her stomach pang, as if she were burying her leavings rather than a precious part of her very being, and the weight of the sand on it chimed through her, as though her shoulders were weighted down. *I'll have to endure it.*

Searching her surroundings, feeling the air currents, Darla

memorised this location. Even though the beach was long, and the stones were liable to be covered and uncovered with the whims of the tide, she did not fret that she would be able to find this exact spot again. She was an expert navigator, one of the best at finding flat fish just from the trails of water over their gills. She would be able to navigate here in full light or night.

Getting to her flippers—feet—she saw how the tide had drained back, taking Neri with it. Her sister's pale head bobbed far out to sea, out of focus. Darla's eyes adjusted to the light, and she could make out her sister's wide black eyes staring at her.

Lifting one of her long limbs, Darla turned and headed straight for the scrub line.

The beach sands were familiar wet, even underneath the pads of these feet, but as she walked up the beach, they became softer, more liable to move and collapse under her. The land gave rather than provided a firm surface. *Not only are surface-dwellers unable to explore upwards, but the ground they are forced to tread is unreliable!* Her muscles worked in unexpected ways, and before long her calf muscles were hurting.

Not sure why they call them calves. Darla rubbed the backs of her sore legs. *They don't look like the young of...*

A sensation like the promise of a riptide dragged at her senses. Closing her eyes, she tried to pinpoint where it had come from. The after echoes faded quicker out in the open than in water, and it was lost before she could determine a direction.

She did feel the ripple of air, a small interruption to the wind. Tracking alongside the scrub, she found a place where the plants bound the soil and extended into the sand, as grasping as the tide in a slow encroachment on the sea's territory and blurring the boundary between land and water.

Her foot touched something round, and she stumbled,

falling to her knees. The fall raised some sand, the wind whipping it into her face. Spitting and scouring her mouth of hair, Darla looked at what she had landed next to.

A human!

Two long legs like hers, two arms, and a head—all intact. Darla had seen enough drowned humans to know that this one was alive; its colour was different, all tans and golds like the sand, with flaring reds in the hair, like the last rays of the summer sun. It wore clothes. A shiny black hide covered its legs, with the sand filling every crease, so Darla left that alone, but on its chest the hide was a different colour. It was open, metal lining the edges of the wound. Her fingers traced it before she snatched her hand away. Perhaps this was how the human had been hurt?

But there was no blood. Darla lowered her head, sniffing, searching for the cause of the human's unconsciousness. The way it lay there, eyes closed, breathing slow, it reminded her of a sleeping seal. It was resting.

She touched the hide on the chest again. This was a red colour, red as a beadlet anemone. Perhaps this was eating the human, digesting it slowly. Fascinating! Darla settled down to watch, but when the hide merely flapped in the wind, she grew bored. Finding a stick, she poked it firmly to see if she could goad it into protecting its meal and doing something interesting.

It failed to do so. Perhaps the human could be woken? As she put her hands to its shoulders, the warnings of the elders filtered down to her.

Humans have caught us to keep us for breeding. Trapped on shore and forced to follow he who holds our skin, made to lie with him and bear his children, half of land and half of the sea, belonging to neither and cast out from both.

Darla shook her head. Her skin was safely buried out of sight, and no one could find it except her. Why would this human suspect that she was not human anyway? Did she not have the correct number of limbs, hair on her head and between her legs, and mammaries? Anyone looking at her would immediately know she was human.

Which was a good thing, because the human was waking up.

CHAPTER 4

Rory

Rory's head hurt. Black and white shapes strode across his vision. Was this death?

Damn, but it hurts too much to be the sweet embrace of oblivion. Bad luck, Rory, this is just a bad trip. Rory struggling to tear through the Veil, but he'd had the starting grace of a permanent portal to help. What did that mean for the state of magic and the realms?

Never mind that right now. I need to feel sorry for myself for a bit. Keeping his eyes closed, he took in the fresh scent of the sea. *Great. Sand will be in every crack and crevice for months to come.* Like any good cat, Rory avoided water as best he could, and especially the sea. It mocked him, he was sure. Ever since he was small, he had carried an inkling that the embrace of death would find him in the fathomless oceans. *If I'd known I was seeing a shipwreck, I would have stayed clear.* No wonder there was a tangle of souls here; lives must have gone down with the ship, causing that pull he felt.

His soul sense tingled, hard. The souls were right there at his elbow. His luck was changing at least. He opened his eyes, and his heart nearly wrenched out of his chest.

"Hello, fellow human!" A naked woman sat at his side.

Scrambling upright, Rory flailed backwards. "What are you?"

The woman's eyes widened. She looked to be on a bad trip all of her own, pupils shrunk to pinpricks. "I am a human! Like you are, of course."

"And I'm also King of the Topaz Court." *What the fuck?* How was she managing to mask her scent like that, and why was she glowing like a uranium rod against his soul sense?

She surged forward, and Rory yelped. His daggers were in the small of his back, no use right now. He put his hands up, but that just meant she pressed her breasts into his open palms as she reached her hands to his hair. Rory tensed for a blow as she ducked her head.

She pressed her cheek to his. The sides of his lips were acutely sensitive; the nerve endings of his whiskers were still there, even if the whiskers weren't in this form. Her head blocked out the whirl of the wind, so that he was surrounded by her skin. Warm, smooth and as soft as the underbelly of a kitten. He smelled the sea on her and through her, a tangy salt on his senses that he knew she would taste of. His tongue flickered out to check...

He snatched at his wits and dumped her to the side. "What are you doing?"

She looked utterly shocked, those pinprick pupils locked on him. "Saying hello."

Scoffing, Rory got to his feet. "Is this your first time in the human realm?"

"I... am clearly a human." She gestured down at herself, cheeks flushing.

Rory averted his gaze, but then again, she had offered. He took a moment to look her up and down. She had a lovely lustre to her skin, gleaming on all her curves, which he could objectively call luscious. Her hair whipped in the wind, shoulder-length fine curls that tangled on her ears and nose like a spring weed. Some wisps brushed her full lips, which parted slightly.

Rory nodded curtly. "Nicely proportioned and all that. What are you supposed to be, mid-twenties? Good-sized hips and…" His palms remembered well the feel of her, of how rounded she was. He swallowed hard.

She inclined her head as she got to her feet. "Thank you." Squinting up at him, she patted his shoulder. "Your fat masses are collected mainly in your shoulders."

"Fat, this is muscle," Rory muttered, slapping his thighs to dislodge the sand. "And if you're going to swan around here, you will need to blend in a bit more."

"Don't I look the same as you?" She put her hands to her face. "But I just came like this! I didn't have any control over where the fat settled!" Do all humans look like you do?"

"No." Rory smirked. "I'm considered a fine specimen."

"Then what am I? Am I not supposed to be like this?"

Rory nearly choked on his laughter. "I have no complaints over the form, myself." *Quite the opposite.* She looked good enough to eat. Putting his hands on his hips, Rory weighed his options. Option one was easy, leave the strange naked thing and go on his way. Whatever she was, she was lost. She would either give up and go back where she came from, or…

Rory's stomach tightened. Something else could find her. There existed the possibility that other, less charitably minded creatures could find her. When he had first become alert, he had been half surprised to still be alive. This plane used to be rife with all kinds of creatures and the gamut of their intentions, from merely mischievous to predatory. If the Cu Sidhe had found Rory, he would have been a pelt on Shay's wall before sundown. She had an amazing signature like a knot of delectable souls and she was conspicuous; a short conversation was enough to ascertain that she wasn't a denizen of this realm and therefore fair game. Heck, even other humans hurt each other, presumably for some kind of sport.

Option two was to instruct her on how to blend in a bit more. Not help, no, because fae never helped. Having the humans swarming around this region excited about fae would definitely hinder whatever Orla's plans were in the move against Shay. It was purely self-interest, therefore, to keep her out of their notice.

And option three was to have a bit of fun with her. She was very handsome looking, whatever her real form was, and Rory was experienced enough to know that even horrendous tentacle monsters could be a really good time. Her true face might pull his mind inside out and back to front, but as long as she stayed civil, he could as well.

"I will offer you a deal," he said. He would have to word this carefully. "I can assist you, and in return, you will—"

"Oh, you'll help me? Wonderful" She sprang up, the motion doing very interesting things to her bosom.

Rory backed away a step, stumbling in the shifting sands. "I said I might, I *could*, if you promise to do something for me in return. That's how deals work." Biting the inside of his cheeks to stop his mouth from running on, he pulled his jacket closed and fastened the zip.

"Fascinating." Clasping her hands in front of her, she tilted her head. "What would you have me do?"

With effort, Rory wrenched his gaze up to her eyes instead of her boobs. *I am being terribly heroic, doing all these good deeds today.* "Oh, I'm sure I'll think of something."

Her eyes narrowed slightly. Brown curls floated in the breeze, obscuring her face for a moment. She bit her lip, digging her fingernails into her palms.

When she swept her head with her forearm, brushing her hair out of the way, her face was pensive. "I'll need something specific, I'm afraid. Open-ended bargains are a good way to get cheated."

Rory tried to think. All he could see was skin and flesh, but it seemed tacky to just demand a tumble. He might if she were flirtatious, but her actions were genuine, and genuinely clueless. She didn't know how inappropriately she was acting; thinking of taking advantage of that left a sick, sour taste in Rory's mouth.

There was always the old fae fallback. A bit unimaginative, but useful, nonetheless. "A favour for the future, then. Something that you will do to help me when the time comes, and I ask for it."

Tucking her hair behind her ear, she stayed quiet. *Her eyes are dark grey.* She was all pale golds, browns, and greys, the colours of autumn.

Her voice rang clearly. "If it is within my power, if it is something I can do, and if it will not hurt me or anyone else to do so, then I will do it." The wind picked up, an eager edge to it, as the residual magic of the land sluggishly wove around their words. Had the human realm suddenly gotten an influx of magic somehow?

Rory held out his hand with a smirk. "Very well."

Her palm slapped his, and she barked with laughter.

Shaking out his hurting hand, Rory frowned. "What was that?"

She held up her hand, then clapped both hands together, giving herself a high five. "It's how you agree a bargain."

Rory shook his head. "That's how you greet friends, at least in the 1980s as time is measured here." Rory frowned, looking over her head at the shore. "That's a point, what era are we? What year is it?"

"Um." She shrank in on herself a little. "By our reckoning, we count the years as one thousand nine hundred and ninety, but it might also be one thousand nine hundred and ninety-nine. An auspicious year, indeed."

Tutting, Rory unzipped his jacket. "First item of business is some clothes. Not that I don't appreciate the view, but clothes are customary in any human region and at any point in human history. You need to stay here while I get you something."

"I don't want to stay here." The woman tiptoed up to his elbow. She was shorter than him, coming up to his shoulder , and she scowled out at the choppy waters. Her odd pinpoint gaze turned up to him, beseeching. "I want to see."

Rory pulled the jacket over her shoulders, then threw his arm wide to encompass the whole desolate horizon. "You can see the sea."

More hair tangled in front of her face. She huffed to blow it free, and before he could think, his fingers were pushing her hair back behind her ear.

She leaned into his hand, rubbing her cheek against his palm and curling her hands into his jacket. "You feel interesting."

Rory snatched his hand back, patting his pockets and then folding his arms across his chest firmly. *Nope, not gonna think about that.* "Never mind, I'll return to this spot in a few hours."

Her eyes widened, perhaps at being left alone. "I will come with you."

"No, you'll cause a stir. You don't feel like you shift into a dog to me, and those are the only animals you can bring into human habitation without drawing attention to yourself." Imagining if she were a cow, Rory snorted at the mental image of himself leading her lowing down the high street and the ruckus that would cause in certain centuries of human history.

She narrowed her eyes at him. "Why don't I want attention? Why is that bad?"

"Attention means someone will impose their agenda on you.

It's better to stay out of the way of anyone with power or authority, and especially anyone with an axe to grind. And as it can be hard to determine who has that, the best option is to stay unremarkable."

As if this creature could stay unremarked upon, anyone speaking to her would know she was not of this realm and surely couldn't help but be drawn to her. The form she was wearing was enticing enough to him. Maybe she was a siren?

Rory forced himself to leave without a backward glance. As he gained the shaggy hills of the sand dunes and started climbing, he allowed himself one look back at her. She sat in the open and, while she had tugged his jacket on, she hadn't secured the fastening, so Rory was teased with her lush form in glimpses just underneath the open zip. Seeing her swamped by his clothing was decidedly... an interesting feeling.

Focus on the way forward. Step one, find out when and where you are, then step two is figure her out. Rory still had those souls to secure. Perhaps there was a car accident just around the corner. That would be convenient.

A brisk five-minute stroll in the biting wind brought him many benefits: cooling his head and his skin, his palms still tingling where he'd had cupfulls of her, and giving him clues as to what decade he found himself in. Over the edge of the dunes was a gravel car park, a very good way of ascertaining his whereabouts in the timeline and in the country. The information board hadn't been updated since the 1960s, but the messages of undying love scrawled in the weathered wood around the edges provided some dating for him as well as some out-of-date dating advice. The board placed him firmly in St Andrews, along the coast of Fife in Scotland. There were no humans about, just a handful of their parked cars, the patterns on the numberplates suggesting late 1980s to early 1990s.

But as to where the recently released souls might be, there were no cairns of flowers, no little plastic-wrapped teddy bears tied to the posts to suggest an accident. *Perhaps there was an accident of some enormity, something that shook the timeline?* Rory had never heard of such a thing, scoffing at himself. Deaths were not like an oil spill, where the effect could be marked in that spot for years to come. The moment of death was instantaneous, a blip. It was the soul that was a tangible thing to the right fae.

Stretching out his senses, he could only feel a pull back to the shoreline. To the new fae?

His skin prickled as a car rolled to a stop beside him. Reflexes eons old made his teeth lengthen and his claws want to shoot out. Whatever was coming next wasn't going to be salubrious.

CHAPTER 5
Darla

Darla had watched the man make his way over the sand dunes. His steps were sure and well-placed. She had had no idea that walking could be so beautiful.

He was beautiful too, a being of hard planes that reminded her of the weather-beaten rocks forming the cliffs of the land. Some were smoothed to benign roundness by the unrelenting waves. Others sheared and broken, leaving jagged edges that cut and speared.

He was dangerous, of that there was no doubt. But he had taken off his thicker clothing and bestowed it upon her, leaving himself with only a thinner material that would not bear the wind for long.

Darla felt the chill on the shore less now that she had his red hide curled around her. Nuzzling her nose deeper into the collar, it smelled of him; deep pheromones that she could untangle and straighten out if she were in the right mind to do so. They were dizzying and confusing, speaking directly to her body and bypassing her conscious thoughts entirely. For example, her legs seemed unstable, when they had been perfectly able to carry her before.

She was glad she was sitting.

Turning her back to the rumble of the outgoing tide, Darla focused on the plants around her. They had bent away from the sea, probably from the unrelenting wind always forcing them to bow over backwards. *Why are you here, on the very edge of this place? So stubborn.* Darla had heard about forests, quiet places with trees overflowing with leaves overhead. No trees grew here, only twisted trunks. *Why not be more inland, where you will be safe and have an easier time of it?*

Scanning over the horizon, Darla saw the human's red hair disappear down the other side of the dunes. Her heart gave a lurch, and she stood up. He said he would be back, but humans could lie. He might not even come back for his hide; it didn't seem to pain him to give it to her, and he hadn't transformed into anything else.

Truly, was he even human? The things he said suggested he was not. What was he, then? Selkies had brought back tales from the land, mentioning all sorts of phenomena, and Darla did not yet know enough to sort human from non-human. He at least seemed helpful, if a little fixed on bargaining and not using proper greetings. Perhaps they said hello differently here. Holding up her hand, she recalled he said that slapping palms was a greeting here, not a way to conclude a bargain. She had so much to learn! Excitement sparked along her newly human skin underneath the borrowed jacket.

Thrilling, and yet here she was, sitting on the shoreline, waiting for him to return. *If* he would return at all. The wind relented, and everything became still and quiet as if silencing for Darla's deliberation. Well, she'd decided; she stood and marched after him.

Darla's cheeks tingled. Something big moved the air currents ahead of her, over the tops of the sand dunes where the man had disappeared. She walked faster, picking her way through the unstable sandy mounds. An unwary step would cause a pile of sand to crumble underneath her. How had the man done it? He had seemed to weave over the tops of the dunes. *There must be some trick to it. I'll have to figure it out or ask him to teach me.* Her skin flushed at the idea of him leaning over her shoulder, holding her hips, murmuring instructions in her ear on where to place her feet and when to shift her weight, nudging her into position...

Finally gaining the top, red-faced and blowing air as if she had resurfaced after a long dive, Darla tasted the wind currents. They had a bitter edge, picking up something oily as they skimmed over the land here. Cars lined up nearby on a cleared parcel of land, and she gasped. She and her sister had explored these on the seabed whenever they came across one. Relics from the human world, their preferred mode of transport rather than using their legs! *I understand why, these legs aren't very resilient over this slippery ground.*

Warm air spilled out of one that vibrated, a low growl that set her hackles on edge. Next to it stood the red-haired man, his hands raised. The sides of the car opened, and three other humans disgorged from it. Well, the required number and shape of heads and limbs to signal humans, but Darla suspected that some beings wore human forms.

Why would a being take the shape of another? In her case, it was curiosity, but she could well imagine it evolving as the perfect means of predation, and all her well-honed senses screamed *predators* as she watched the trio face off against the human she had found in the sands.

He clearly viewed them as a threat, baring his teeth but not making any move to run. He might be hurt or tired, unable to risk fighting. If he didn't make them leave or vacate the area, Darla feared the predators would strike.

Three faced him, two with short hair and one with longer

hair and prominent mammaries like hers. Her eyes focused on the flashes in their hands, like they held shards of sunlight. They were holding knives.

"Ruairí." The one in front spoke, kicking the sides of the car he had arrived in as he sauntered around it. "Thought I sensed you here."

The man from the shore—this Ruairí—inclined his head. "I'd say it was good to see you again, Akir, except we both know that's a lie. I assure you, I am here by accident, and I'll be leaving shortly."

"You'll be leaving, alright. A head shorter, too." The leader, Akir, laughed.

Darla did not like that laugh. She started running toward them.

A tactic when faced with a predator was to attack directly, especially if a member of the colony was injured. This gave the others time to escape and was often not anticipated by the predator. The woman spotted her first, but Darla's sudden appearance made her take a step back rather than toward her.

Akir turned, fists raised, then he smirked. "Hello, darling." He frowned. "Hey, does she have anything on her muff—"

Swooping into the opening, Darla grabbed his head and sank her teeth into his ear. Screaming, Akir raked her back with his hands and something sharp slid down her spine. She tasted blood as her jaws ratcheted closed. Akir shoved her hard, but Darla held on. "Get her off, get her off!"

The larger man came behind her, and Darla tensed for a blow, but the red-haired human launched himself in between them, throwing wild punches. Then the woman entered the fray, swinging at Darla's head. A knife flashed, and Darla shut her eyes tight.

Darla let go and dropped to the floor.

The woman's knife plunged into Akir's cheek. With a wild shriek, the man staggered back, pressing a hand to his face.

Ruairí started laughing.

"Oh crap!" The woman backed away, hands to her face.

Akir reeled, holding onto his bleeding face. "Stupid cow! Get her! Kill them both!"

Darla rolled away from stomping feet, barrelling into the larger man. He went down but spun around faster than she would have thought humans could move. She screamed, lunging for him with jaws wide, and the larger man scrabbled backwards.

"Stop trying to bite them!" Ruairí was doubled over, barely able to breathe through the laughter.

Darla snapped her teeth at the larger man. "It's effective, is it not?"

Drawing a wickedly curved blade, the large man slashed down. Darla jerked her legs out of the way, but it caught her calf, slicing with red-hot pain.

Ruairí sprouted fur all over and seized the larger man in his claws, ripping and rending at his clothes. Behind him, the leader and the woman had regrouped; pressing his hand to his cheek, the leader raised another nasty serrated blade. Darla tackled him around the waist, wincing as that knife came down. It glanced to the side, scraping along her ribs on her right side. *This red pelt must be very thick to offer such protection!*

"Get her off me!" Akir screamed.

"We need to get out of here!" the woman replied.

Kicking Darla off, the leader spat, "You might have won this round, but you mark my words, Rory, I'll hang you by the hide and skin you alive!"

Ruairí raised a small ball, shining like a pearl but as big as her palm, and crushed it between his palms. A curious shimmer appeared in the air underneath their foes and warmth flooded over Darla's cheeks, the wind moving in an erratic way, pulling the air from this world into it like a whirlpool. Akir and the woman vanished into it, and the larger man looked back and forth between Ruairí and the strange mouth in the floor. Ruairí puckered his lips at him, and the man ran into the shimmer to disappear as well.

Darla rubbed her cheeks, keen to erase that strange feeling, and when she tentatively lowered her hands the sensation had disappeared. "Where did they go?"

Ruairí sucked in ragged breaths. The fur, red like the hair on his head, slowly faded to leave a bristle on his jaw and claws slowly retracted into his lengthening fingertips.

Humans don't do that. She peered closer as he wiped his hands on the grass, leaving an oily glimmer that evaporated.

Straightening up from his crouch, he ran his fingers through his hair, settling and smoothing it. "I catapulted those redcaps into the fae realm. Akir might be back to defend his territory, perhaps with more friends, so we should get somewhere more populated. They aren't allowed to accost fae in sight of humans..." He trailed off, nose twitching, then twisting around. "You're hurt!" he accused.

"Am I?" Darla stretched her legs out in front of her. The long slice in her calf bled, but she could flex her leg at least. Now that the fight was over, it hurt with a pounding sting, like a jellyfish tendril had wrapped around it. "Oh, yes."

Ruairí hunkered next to her, knees pressing against the hard. Hovering his hands over the wound, he asked, "May I touch you, to dress and bind it?"

Darla's heart was already racing, but it gave a lurch. "Yes."

He glanced up into her eyes, assessing. "I'd say you were suffering from shock, but your pupils have always been small."

"My... pupils?"

Nodding, the man unbuttoned his shirt. It was a very light grey like her sister's pelt, but his tan skin was a warm brown more like hers. Each button slipped free, revealing wide muscle crowned with pink nipples, and then tapering sharply to a pebbled stomach with ridge lines as if the tide had marked him, the muscle rippling as he moved. Red hair dusted a pathway from his navel to his trouser band, which sat low on his hips.

He was speaking to her. "They allow light into your eyes. I'd say you lived somewhere very dark normally, to have them adjust like that."

Darla didn't understand what he was talking about at first. "Oh, the pupils." Touching her eyelids, she exhaled. Focus!

When she lifted her head, she was confronted by his bare shoulder. He shucked his shirt free, then lifted it. The shapes she had taken for fat deposits at his shoulders were pure muscle, standing proud in the air as he tore his shirt clean in half. Laying the ruined cloth against her injured calf, he pressed down hard and used another scrap to tie the bandage down.

"There. Now." The man sat back on his heels. "This is where you tell me you can heal yourself quicker than blinking."

Darla's throat loosened. "That would be helpful, but that only happens by the hand of the one who hurt me."

His head jerked up. "Well, I'll track the bastard down and cut his hand off."

She grabbed his forearm. "No, no, it has to be attached. And the intent to heal the harm caused must be sincere."

The man clucked his tongue. "Give me a week, he'll be selfishly sincere," he said, low voice dark. He looked down at her hand, then back up along her arm. "The jacket deflected the worst of it, at least. Who taught you how to fight by biting people? That's a terribly vulnerable way to fight."

Darla shrugged, ducking her head into the collar. Tiredness dragged at her limbs, and she closed her gritty, dry eyes.

CHAPTER 6
Rory

The woman looked utterly drained. Her golden skin shone with a fine sheen of sweat, and her eyes lacked their bright lustre.

Rory surveyed car park, deserted for now with no humans about. That was why the redcaps had felt comfortable about attacking.

Stretching out his limbs, he winced. He would suffer minor bruises, his jaw aching a little where his teeth had forced it to strain. That was what happened if one part-shifted, but dying on the dunes on a redcap's blade wasn't on his to-do list today.

The woman hadn't moved, crouching into his jacket. It swamped her, a fact she was probably grateful for. The metal sewn into the back had saved her life. *Good.* Hunkering down next to her, Rory tried to gauge her condition. "Can you walk a few steps? We're going to take their car, get us some new clothes, and find something to eat."

Nodding once, she struggled to her feet. Rory held out his arms, but she did not take them. She shuffled to the car, whose engine still purred, and touched its roof. She looked over her shoulder at him, a quiet question in her eyes.

"You climb inside and sit. Here, it's perfectly safe." Rory demonstrated, sitting in the passenger seat.

She nodded again, and Rory stood to let her in. Her gaze traced his chest as he rose in front of her, before her face tipped up to look into his eyes, something of her former sparkling energy coming back to her features and her cheeks flushing with interest.

If she was drawn to him, that would be a mistake on her part. He pointed to the car seat. "After you."

She sat, and Rory leaned over her to secure her seatbelt. His hands warmed close to her bare hip, acutely aware that she was naked underneath his jacket. He wiped his shaking hands on his trousers. *Keep it together, for fae's sake!* It was not as if he was a teenager again—that had been a hard century and a half— but he could recognise the effect of post battle endorphins. Rather like the high after an orgasm, producing some kind of bonding chemical... that's all this was.

Looking in the back of the car yielded three suitcases of clothes. The redcap Akir had taken a body only a little taller than Rory so his stuff would fit, and he had expensive tastes. He held up a black shirt. *This will do nicely.* Buttoning it up, Rory flicked through the woman's clothes.

"Here." Sitting in the driver's seat, Rory passed over a bundle of clothes, jeans and a few tops.

She took the bundle carefully. "Where did you get these from?"

"The redcaps, those things we fought, they must have stolen this vehicle and the forms they wore from some humans recently."

She cocked her head. "How do you know?"

"That they were redcaps? The smell." Nose wrinkling, Rory gagged. "You can smell their forest from our castle when the wind is in the wrong direction. Akir and his gang create pools of blood, it's their... *hobby.*" His lips twisted. "That's how I know they've killed only recently, too; it's not like redcaps to have so many clean clothes. Usually, they dye them red with the blood of their victims."

The woman's eyes went wide, and Rory bit his tongue. Grasping onto the steering wheel, he adjusted the rear-view mirror. "Sorry. I should have probably kept that tidbit to myself."

"No. I want to know everything there is to know," she whispered. "Although... I do kind of wish I didn't know that." She stroked the bundle of clothes.

"Well, knowledge is a burden and all that." Rory watched her hand. She was shaking. "You might as well have the clothes. It's not like the owner will miss them."

"I suppose." Holding them to her face, she took a deep sniff. "I can smell the human who owned these. They... they liked plants. Something sweet. I don't recognise the smell."

So, her key sense was smell as well. Leaning over, Rory took in a breath, inhaling a salt scent of the sea. Underneath that was washing powder, and... "Lilies. Poisonous to cats." Rory grimaced. "Ah well, not everyone is a cat lover, I suppose."

"How do I...?" The woman held up the jeans helplessly, turning the leg this way and that.

Dressing a woman in a car was a new experience for Rory and a reversal of the usual procedure, but she needed to dress before they went somewhere more crowded. "Put your legs through the waistband here, like that. Now one leg in each... tube, I suppose. Good."

She beamed with the praise, some kind of golden light shifting under her skin, as if she radiated happiness.

Rory found his lips curving up into a smile. "That's it. Now lift your hips, and..." Rory stared as she arched her back. *Naked, remember.*

"Now... pull these up?" She guessed.

"I, uh, what? No. Yes! I mean yes." Gripping the steering

wheel hard, Rory scanned the beach car park again. *Cold water. Very cold water, middle of the North Sea cold.* Dark depths below surging, relentless waves eroding him, death claiming him...

Once icy calm had subdued his rather excited frame of mind, Rory dared to turn back.

Now she had his jacket off and wrestled with a cropped top, her arms helplessly tangled over her head and breasts bare.

"Damnation, woman. You'll be the death of me," Rory muttered, sinking his head into his hands.

She squeaked. "Help?"

"I... yes." Soft, tan skin called to him, but Rory managed to tug and pull the fabric only, helping her settle it over her assets. The top showed off her muscled shoulders and firm stomach.

She flashed a small gap between her two front teeth in a grateful smile. "Thank you. I'm Darla."

The sluggish magic of the land pinged at him. "Your true name? How trusting, and rather naive. With that, I could have complete command over you." *Cold seas. Freezing waves. Damnation!*

Her face fell a little. "Oh. Was that wrong of me?"

Rory inhaled. "Any fae would take advantage of that, but luckily, I haven't had caffeine yet, so we will take care of that before I think of some nefarious purpose to put you to."

Tugging at her hair, pulling it over the straps of the black crop top, she smiled. She clearly didn't believe him.

"That's a serious threat, I'll have you know." Rory tried to sound menacing and not petulant. He gave up. "You can call me Rory."

"Oh. Those redcaps called you Ruairí. Is that your real name?"

Rory flinched as his true name rolled over her lips. "Ah. You're rather attentive."

With a flash of those teeth in a wickedly curved smile, she hummed. "So, I could command *you*, if I wanted to."

A streak of desire uncurled in his core. *Ice in the sea. Being dragged down by a whirlpool, sirens grabbing his arms and legs, and...*

Shit.

Coughing to clear his throat, Rory threw the car into gear. Wheels spinning and spitting gravel, the car lurched forward and Darla was thrown back into her seat with a cry, clinging onto his hand on the gearstick.

"I need my hand to operate the gearstick. I suppose you can hold it if you want, as long as you don't interfere with my movements."

"Yes." As they sped out of the car park, she twisted to look back out of the rear window.

"What is it?" Rory barked. Had the redcaps returned?

"Nothing," she whispered, her grey eyes wide as they turned out of the junction and onto the main road. "I just can't see the sea anymore."

She settled into quiet and Rory was content to let her and retreat to his own thoughts, but her reticence was short lived. She asked unending questions about the most asinine and mundane things. "What is this?" "What is that?" "What does that do?" Inside or outside the car, her attention jumped from one thing to the next. Rory found himself explaining tarmac and how it was called asphalt elsewhere on Earth, what the white lines symbolised, what a sign indicated, how the air conditioning worked and why the engine was making that noise when he ground the gearbox. He was rusty on driving a manual—or stick shift—and the steering wasn't assisted with power, so his guess that he had landed in the late 20th century seemed more and more likely. If only there was a way to be sure before he interacted with any humans...

He nearly smacked himself in the forehead and turned on the radio. Music flooded the car, and Rory nearly groaned.

Darla's latest question died on her lips, and she whipped

around in her seat. "Where is that music coming from? Are there sirens?" she shouted.

Wincing, Rory turned the volume down. "Worse. The Spice Girls. We are indeed in the height of the 1990s. Great."

"Oh, good." She did not seem to understand sarcasm.

In between keeping an eye on the road conditions, Rory stole sideways glances at her. Her quick gaze took in the land-scape flickering by, her wild brown curls caressing her shoulders as she turned her head this way and that. She inhaled deeply, eyes half-lidding as if in ecstasy, and Rory was struck with an image of her wearing that expression, lying sated on his bed...

Sharks in the water too. Biting me all over and tearing me to pieces. But it wasn't having any effect on calming his reaction to her magnetic effect.

Checking the road signs, Rory settled onto a dual carriage-way, waiting for the music on the radio to turn into a news program so he could zero in on the exact date. "So, you know some sirens, then?"

Scowling, she straightened in her seat. "We keep them out of our territory, but yes. They have gotten more desperate recently, though, and even tried attacking the colony a few full moons ago. We saw them off, but they looked rather thin and haggard. I almost felt sorry for them."

"You sound like there's no love lost between you." If she hated sirens, what type of fae might she be? A lot of the fae born and raised on Earth were fairly feral, surviving from meal to meal and not particularly intelligent. Darla was well-spoken and sounded educated, but at the same time, she found this realm a marvel. She might be from the fae-realm, except she didn't smell like it.

Darla scowled. "I don't agree with the sirens' methods. Bewitching a human to drown themselves, that's awful. I know they have to eat, but why not diversify the diet? They won't eat drowned people they just find in the sea, which is silly. It's still the same, after all."

"What do you eat?" Rory asked carefully.

She flashed him that gap-toothed smile. "I don't eat you, never fear." Leaning forward in her seat, she rested her chin on her hands. Those golden eyes focused on him, the attention acute, as if he were the only thing in the vicinity. Fields and forests flashed by, and she gave them no mind. "You can take the form of a cat, can't you? I've heard about them. I've never met one, though."

Telling a strange fae what he was would be tactically disadvantageous. It would be disastrous if she were an ally of the Cu Sidhe, and although Rory was fairly certain she wasn't one of those, he still couldn't guess what type of fae she was. She smelled like a fae of the sea, and as far as Rory was concerned, if it smelled like a duck, it was a duck, no further questions. His nose had never failed him.

Thinking she might be more open if he responded, Rory finally nodded. "A Cat Sidhe. Soul stealers, if you want to be offensive. And you are?"

Pulling her legs up underneath her, she tucked her hair behind one ear. "I don't think I can say. I'm not supposed to be here for long."

"Well, neither am I." Rory grinned at her, but inside he was tense. "I won't tell if you won't."

She frowned at him, as if she sensed the lie.

"I could make you tell," he said, flexing his hands on the steering wheel. "I could compel you, Darla." He let the syllables of her name roll around on his tongue. They tasted... good. New. Interesting.

Her skin pebbled with goosebumps as she felt the effect of her true name. Cocking her head, she settled her hands in her lap. "I don't think you will," she said quietly.

"Oh?"

"You could have done so rather than just threatening me with it. I don't think you want to compel me to do anything."

Rory shifted up, pressing his foot against the accelerator. Her words chimed as truth, and that unsettled him. Of course, he would and could compel anyone, once he had the power of their true name or a leverage over them, to achieve his objectives. "What I *want* has nothing to do with it. I just could." Rory turned his attention to overtaking an eighteen-wheeler, streaking into the oncoming lane and shifting down. The engine squealed.

Darla held onto the dashboard. "Don't you get to choose what you do?"

"Of course." The driver of the lorry laid on the horn; there were oncoming vehicles in the road ahead, windscreens flashing in the sun. "I always have options."

Darla looked at him. "Then what you want is very relevant." She sunk lower into her seat.

Rory shifted gears, slammed his foot on the accelerator, and swerved back into the correct lane, just as the blue Ford opposite them sounded their horn. The driver hadn't been about to stop either, though.

Cranking her neck backwards, Darla released the dashboard. "Was that some kind of territory thing?"

"Hm?"

Her nose wrinkled. "It had to be a display of some kind."

"What are you talking about?"

"That manoeuvre. There was nowhere else for the cars to go except directly at each other, but it seemed that whoever backed down first would lose." She cocked her head. "I should think that two of these things impacting each other would cause a lot of damage to their carapace. It was potentially costly."

"Look, I just overtook a lorry on a single carriageway. Not rocket science."

"Hm." She tapped her lip. "Maybe a mating ritual..." she murmured to herself.

Rolling his eyes, Rory leaned on the accelerator again. What had they been talking about?

Ah, yes. Wants and choices. Options. Rory always had options. And right now, he chose to take them out of redcap hell and into somewhere a little more civilised. Once he had had something to eat and taken in some of the concentrated magic to regain a little energy, he would be able to tear the Veil again and get back to the fae realm. Orla would be disappointed he hadn't found any souls and loathe to give him more magic, but the stunt he had pulled dumping the redcaps back where they belonged had cost him dearly, and he couldn't continue a search without enough magic to defend himself. Before then, he could give this creature a briefing so she could stay inconspicuous.

A small beacon of civilisation greeted him and, flipping on the indicator, he eased them off the faster road and crawled into the car park. "First stop. Shit coffee, but decent food."

Darla peered out of the window at the huge, smiling mascot. "What's this?"

"Roadside cafe." Pulling to a stop, Rory reached over her knees and opened the glove box and immediately she swarmed her hands in, curious and touching everything, including the back of his hands.

He sighed, her cold fingers pushing past his. "Will you give me a minute? I'm looking for some cash."

"What is this?" She practically breathed it, all hushed and reverent. "Treasure?"

What kind of creature was she? Where did she come from, and what was she doing here? None of it was truly Rory's concern, of course, but she was intriguing. A mystery, maybe even something new under the sun he hadn't seen before.

She *had* been helpful. Rory admitted that the fight with the redcaps could have gone poorly, given their numbers and his relative strength at the time. She had put herself at risk with no knowledge that the jacket would have afforded her some protection.

Why had she done that?

A strange creature indeed.

CHAPTER 7

Darla

The Cat Sidhe, whatever one of those was, was proving to be a strange creature. His attitude was one she would have called aloof in a selkie male visiting her colony, thinking himself too good for the females surrounding him. Darla hated any pandering to egos and refused to do it, letting only the silly females feel the pressure from the elders. If those males were solely what she had to choose from, then no wonder.

At first, it seemed this Rory would be like that, until he showed care and concern, perhaps even protectiveness, and he answered her myriad questions readily. A pang of regret over not telling him her true nature slid through her; he had been open with her. It seemed the selkie leader's warning had apparently woven its way into her head and made her reticent.

The door next to her opened , the wind whipping her hair into her face. This air smelled of something heavy and burnt, and Rory braced the door against the current to keep it open for her. "Can you walk?"

Darla stared at him stupidly before she remembered. "Oh! The knife wound."

"Yes, the knife wound." His brows drew down. He was displeased. *Why?* "I'll pull you up. Try not to limp. Lean into me if you need to; we can pretend we're a couple."

His outstretched hand waited patiently for hers. Scars crossed the palm like new lifelines. What had his lifelines said of his future, and what did the scars from his past overlay on top of that?

"Well? Are you coming?" There was a hint of amusement in his upturned lips. "I won't bite, unlike you."

Darla put her hand in his. "Don't cats bite?"

He pulled her to her feet. Stretching out her calf did hurt, and she gasped with pain. He gathered her close, warmth through his shirt pressing against her stomach. Her lips and cheeks felt warm too, despite the wind blowing across them.

She didn't dare look up at him. He was something bewitching, for sure. Everything from his body to his voice was alluring. "Can you put weight on it?" he asked, and the words and the timbre and the vibrations in his chest to hers made her feel... good.

Very good.

"I'll try." Darla eased her foot down to the ground.

"Wait." His voice again. She shivered. "I forgot shoes. Stay there for a moment."

Rory left her standing to retrieve something from the tail of the car, two white canvas foot coverings. Darla recognised them from the humans they had seen at a distance.

"Shoes." Rory knelt on the ground in front of her. "Lift your foot. There." Guiding her foot into the shell of the shoe, he went on, "Used by humans pretty ubiquitously to protect their delicate little feet. Different shapes have different purposes. These look like they would be suitable for sport, but they are actually a status symbol." He tied a ribbon to fasten them with quick movements, then beckoned for her other foot.

As she put her full weight onto her injured leg, it wavered.

She locked her knees out as Rory leapt to his feet, catching hold of her shoulders.

"Are you alright?" Now his voice was tender, even though his brows were lowered.

"I... yes." Cat Sidhe must have different body language, different signs and signals. They were bound to. It would be easier if they could touch whiskers, a whole barrage of information could be exchanged that way but this staring into his eyes was also nice...

He blinked slowly, then looked at the shoe in his hand. "Sit in the car seat if you can't put weight on it, and I'll shoe your other foot."

"No, I can do it." Bracing against the pain, Darla shifted her body weight again. This time it hurt but did not give. "There."

"I'll be quick." True to his word, he secured the shoe to her foot, and then stood to hold her hips. "There."

Low levels of discomfort radiated from her leg, more than balanced out by the acute awareness of his body against hers. "Thank you."

He took that as some kind of signal to drop his hands. "My pleasure."

Darla felt the lack of contact but reined herself in. These were all different signals and behaviours to observe and catalogue, not be ensnared by. She had a mere one week to learn everything she could; her body was surely soaking everything in from this man, and she wanted to feel and contemplate it all, not have the experiences rush by.

Rory jerked his head toward the squat solid building emitting curious fumes. He waved at the surface between them and the door, only a handful of strides. "Now then. How do you want to try walking?"

That sparked a question. "How do humans usually walk together?"

He smirked. "Depends on the relationship, and individual

dynamics matter too. Families can be hugging and friends hanging on each other's arms, or be somewhat distant from each other." He shrugged a shoulder, but Darla sensed something else there. *Not a lie, but a hidden story.* "In this instance, in order to provide your leg with some assistance, we should probably choose the guise of lovers."

Now why does that send a shiver down my spine? It had to be the way Rory's breath brushed and tangled with the sensitive places on her cheeks, with his lips so close to her forehead.

A trickle of heat worked its way through her stomach. "How..." Her voice came out choked, as if her throat was full.

Noticing her voice—because of course he would, he was standing so close!—his gaze flickered between her eyes and her lips, settling on her eyes once again. He had a piercing gaze, one that Darla would associate with a lieutenant from another colony: weighing and judging, trying to determine where everyone was in the hierarchy without spending time with them. Quick to come to conclusions, using only what he could see to guide his assessments.

His irises were a golden brown, like her own pelt except shot through with red. But there was a sadness behind his eyes: a deep aching loneliness, a heavy burden, a terrible loss perhaps.

Now *she* was judging by merely what she could see.

She tried again. "How would we do that?"

Grabbing his jacket out of the car, Rory held it out for her. Once she'd slid her arms in, he snaked his arm over her left shoulder and then down her back, tucking the jacket close to her right side. "There, now I'm not touching you directly, but I can still provide you with support. If I forget myself and my hands wander, there's a spare dagger in the breast pocket. I... am not going to pat it to tell you where it is. You'll have to feel around and find it for yourself."

Left arm pressed to his chest, Darla found it more than a

little uncomfortable to try to walk. "What do I do with the arm closest to you?"

Those golden eyes danced. "Well, you have my full permission to wrap that around my lower back. Why not cop a feel as you go? Then you can hold on to this ab, right here." He poked his stomach.

"If you're sure..." Darla's cheeks felt hot, like water needed to rush over them to cool them. Did humans overheat?

Leaning into the experience, Darla traced her arm around his back. He stood, patient and enduring as she placed her hand precisely where he had indicated. Underneath her hand, his muscles shifted.

She squinted up at him. "Are you doing that on purpose?"

Laughing, he took a step. "Perhaps."

Darla hopped after him. "How remarkable. I wonder if I can control my body like that."

"Muscle movement is mainly involuntary, after a certain age." He hoisted her closer. "Nevertheless, I do have a few party tricks. I can flex and show with the best of them." As if to prove it, the hard muscle under her hand jumped again.

Darla barked. "Stop it, you'll give me the giggles."

"Giggles?" His lower lip protruded, and he clutched her close again as she took another halting step.

"Yes!" Darla's good ankle turned, plucking away her balance. She fell.

Rory snatched her up, pressing her back to his chest. She could feel his heart as a rapid tattoo even through the jacket, and his voice was lower when he spoke. "Are you alright?"

"I... definitely don't have the giggles now." Darla gulped in air. Oh, she was definitely attracted to him, her mind racing. How would that work between them?

They managed to make it into the building without further incident, with Rory casting sidelong looks at her leg as if it annoyed him. Darla tried to hobble faster and he kept her steady, not rushing her. The inside of the building was thick with a heavy scent, something that made her nose tingle unpleasantly but her stomach growl possessively. The space was lined with long, shiny, thin platforms surrounded by regular shapes.

"Tables! And chairs."

He smiled down at her, the affection in his gaze making her heart surge.

A tired looking woman hailed them. "Table for two?"

"Please. Secluded, if you will." Rory brought Darla's hand to his lips, placing a soft kiss on the back of it.

Darla's mouth dropped. The warm press of his lips sent a bubble of excitement in her stomach, and it let her feel not only his lips but the sensitive nodes where his whiskers would have been

Smile fixing, the woman pointed to a table alongside the window. "Best we can do, love."

Love? Wasn't that a special term here? And yet this woman handed it out casually. *Interesting.*

"Good, we'll take it. I'm afraid my fiancée's leg took rather a bash on the dunes. Do you have a first aid kit?"

"Err... sure. Disabled toilet." She raised the other arm this time, seemingly exhausted by the motion. "I'll check on you in five, alright?"

"Of course." Grabbing Darla firmly, Rory helped her into a smaller room, pulling a cord to activate a blinding light.

"Ouch." Turning her head up, Darla tried to look directly at it but had to shield her face with a hand. She blinked at Rory with watering eyes.

"Not a fan of electric light?" He pulled a green box from the wall and opened it with a faint hissing sound, sorting through the contents presumptuously in front of a shiny surface that reflected copies of them back at her. Her double winced and ducked her head, but she looked very human; a thrill went through her. *I wish I could capture this image of myself for all time.*

"Gauze, bandages... antiseptic. Good. Now then." He pressed some metal so water gushed out of the tap, then began scrubbing and cleaning the sink and counter. Darla stared at the high pressured water tumbling out and swirling down a hole.

He rested his hands on the counter, meeting her eyes in the shiny surface even though she was behind his shoulder. The intense red in his irises sent a pleasant warmth through her. "You have to bandage that leg. Do you know how?" he said.

She eyed the supplies he had laid out, picking up a metal container. Pulling off the lid, she winced at the strong scent reminding her of emissions from some of those boats. "Do I... eat what's inside this?"

He took it from her. "That's a no." Sighing, he ran a hand through his hair. "I doubt you can roll that trouser leg up either; the shirt is still wrapped around the muscle..." He folded his arms. "You'll have to pull your trousers down."

"Very well." Darla fiddled with the button at her hips on the jeans.

Rory turned away, facing the tiled wall. "Let me know when you're decent. When you've... uh, when you've got the trousers off and covering your... uh, your..." His shoulders shivered.

"My what?" Darla cocked her head at his back.

"You know," he said.

Darla shook her head. "You need the calf uncovered but something else covered. That's all I know. What should be covered?" Pulling down the trousers, she stepped out of them.

"Your nether regions. Those are private and seen by very few people, only those lucky enough to, uh..." His ears were flushing a pretty shade of crimson, like the pink painted top shell. Why was he flushing over some skin showing now when he had seen her completely naked before?

Whatever the reason, it made her smile. "Very well." It was a good phrase. She held the jeans up and pressed them between her legs. "How is this?"

He glanced over his shoulder, back hunched as though waiting for a blow, then turned around fully. The flush spread to his throat and ears. He was attracted too! What had he said about someone being lucky enough?

"Right, now... Stand still." He squatted, and Darla could hear the creak of his clothes. This room was so quiet and immediate, just them, together. He placed his hands on her leg, his palms warm and big, as if they had sprouted fur and turned into paws again. Looking up, his eyes searched hers. "You are very cold. Are you alright?"

"I think that's my normal temperature." She laid the back of her hand on his cheek.

"That's far too cold!" Muttering, he took her hand and chafed it. "One thing at a time. I'm going to wash this out and apply antiseptic, then we will bandage it, and then you are wearing my jacket to keep you warm."

This he did, taking strips of cloth and soaking them in warm water, then gently wiping around the knife wound. He squeezed some of the metal container onto his fingertips, his eyes intent and focused on his work. Darla watched his expressions chase themselves across his face: concern, with his eyebrows raised, then perhaps anger, with the eyebrows lowering and shading his eyes. Wrapping fresh white linen around her calf, the room now smelled of something oily, a harsh taste in the back of Darla's throat. He straightened up, eyes flashing. "I know I'm giving off anger vibes, but I'm not angry at you. I'm incensed with those redcaps and I'll take it out on them, next time we cross paths." Turning away, he washed his hands at the sink. "Get dressed and let's get something to eat."

Darla did so, pulling on and secured her jeans just as the

door shook with a bang. "All okay in there?" The woman's voice chirped.

Darla gave Rory a questioning look. "She thinks we might have our hands all over each other in here," Rory explained.

"We did."

Rory chuckled, and Darla's heart lifted. He was lovely when he laughed. Rory flicked something on the door handle and pulled it open to the disgruntled woman. "Thanks, we are ready to be seated now. Come along, Darla darling."

As they followed the woman, Darla leaned into him. "Darla *darling*?"

He shrugged the shoulder furthest from her. "Not very imaginative, I know. Humans tend to like simple patterns, whether with words, colours or numbers." He lowered his head and his voice, his breath tickling her ear. "They only see seven colours. They are rather limited."

"Oh," Darla murmured, and that kept her mind racing over the revelation—the poor things!—until they were shown to a table.

"Is this all for us?" she asked, jaw dropping.

"See anyone else here today, love?" The woman's smile fixed. "Any drinks to start?"

Rory helped Darla to a seat. "Coffee, strong enough for the spoon to stand unaided. Water."

She nodded and ambled away, and Darla watched her slow steps up to the counter, where she pushed some protrusions and pulled some levers.

Rory's tap on the table brought Darla's attention swinging back to him. "It's considered rude to stare at humans. Now, then. Can you read?"

"Read?" Darla looked over at the paper Rory had in his hands. Coloured pictures decorated it. "What are these?"

"Food. Of a sort. I recommend the All-Day Breakfast; that's at least recognisable. Eggs, bacon, beans. Toast."

The unfamiliar words clashed against Darla's ears. "I will have one of everything."

Rory smirked. "Sure, courtesy of the redcaps." He tapped the table again.

The woman returned with a tray and some containers, setting them out and asking, "What will you be having?"

"Two All-Day Breakfasts, all the trimmings." Rory glanced at Darla. "Side of chips and a milkshake."

"Chocolate, vanilla, or strawberry?" the waitress asked, as if the question drained her.

"Chocolate," Darla said. She clutched the tabletop. "I've never had it, and I've heard so much about it!"

Rory frowned at her, the woman raising her eyebrows. "Chocolate milkshake it is." She shuffled off.

Reaching over, Rory took her hand. "Can you try not to be weird around the humans?"

She pressed her lips together to stop her excitement from bubbling out.

He sighed. "You can be as weird as you like around me, I suppose."

Darla clutched his hand. "Chocolate! Real, actual chocolate!"

He chuckled. "It's Frankenstein cousin in a place like this, but sure." He dropped his chin in his hand. "Where are you from that you've never had chocolate before? Even the fae realm imports that."

She didn't say anything in return. She couldn't, her stomach churning.

He let her hand go. "Can't say or won't say. Hm. I don't smell a compulsion on you."

Darla tensed. He could smell her, which meant he might be able to tell what she was. "It's not important. I promise I don't mean any harm."

He tipped his head to the side. "Yes, I can see that. And I can also see you can take care of yourself, to a great degree." He folded his arms across his chest, making his biceps look bigger in way Darla's body found drawing. She couldn't help but stare, to feel his effect on her, all new experiences to be had. He saw her stare and smirked. "You like?" He made them tense and relax, a bulge that eased up and down his upper arm. It was mesmerising.

Darla giggled, hiding her teeth with her hand so he wouldn't think she was threatening him.

A smile creased his face as he ran a hand through his red hair. "You're strangely naive and yet not at the same time. You practically attacked those redcaps on sight."

Shrugging one shoulder as she had seen him do, Darla smiled back. "You think I cannot tell who the sharks are? They were circling you."

"Sharks, eh." Tapping his lip, he closed his eyes. "But you can still get into trouble if you don't know what you're doing."

"Then I'd like to learn as much as I can, please." She put her head in her hand, mimicking him. "Tell me everything."

He raised an eyebrow. "Everything? Where to start." He drummed his fingers on the table. "I'll start with the most pressing matter. Magic is draining out of the fae realm. There's a hole somewhere, or maybe it's seeping out of the pores of reality; whatever it is, there's less and less to go around every mortal year."

Darla sat forward. "Magic is... leaving?"

He shook his head once. "That implies it has agency. Magic just is; it's a force. It's like gravity or momentum or the sun's rays. But unlike those, it's leeching away, becoming less and less concentrated in the air and water and soil. It makes it harder for beings like me and, I assume, you, to exist."

Darla slowly nodded. Selkie scouts reported the air feeling heavier, the waters thicker near the shores. "I thought that was to do with human activities, they are constantly dropping their leavings everywhere."

"Perhaps." He stared off to one side, as if considering the idea. "Nonetheless, that doesn't change the fact that it's happening, and we have to adapt to it. It's harder and harder to charge gemstones, for example."

Darla opened her mouth to ask questions about gemstones, but then their food arrived. Darla's jaw slackened, her stomach gurgling, as steaming plates piled high with shades of caramel, brown, and red were placed in front of them. She trembled, waiting for the woman handing them this largesse to leave so Rory could explain how to eat it.

Once the woman was gone, Rory handed Darla two metal tools. He held up his own, one in each hand, and used one to chase the food and the other to block its progress. He sawed off a morsel, speared it, and ate it. Darla watched his jaw muscles tighten and relax.

Darla brought the food to her lips. It smelled incredible. Placing it on her tongue, she closed her eyes to savour it. She nearly fell from her seat when the woman returned. "Here's the chocolate milkshake." She set it in front of Darla.

Shaking, Darla put her hands around the glass. It was cold, so cold, a deep brown that had purple tones, like dulce seaweed. It smelled sweet, a cloying scent that confused her senses. It was everywhere all at once.

"Are you going to stare at it or try it?" Rory asked, gently teasing.

"I definitely want to try it, but I want to savour it." Scenting deeply, she let each note settle into her memory: the glass as high as her hand; the brown froth within, sweet and cloying; and over the rim of the glass, Rory's sardonic smirk marring his handsome face. Red hair curled at the edges of his temples and his eyebrows were slightly askew. A scar cut through the one on his left side, only a small silver thing that she never would have noticed had she not been intently memorising him...

He set his elbows on the table. "Take a picture. It'll last longer."

"A picture?" Darla frowned.

He sighed. "Ah, yes. Selectively naïve. A picture is an imprint, a permanent still record."

Darla felt her face warm again. Silly human faces. "I would like to take this picture." She could study it at leisure, although an imprint wouldn't capture his constant movement, his fidgeting from one state to another; sardonic to open, laughing to serious. He was as changeable as the wind.

Rory laughed, a low noise that warmed Darla to her core. "I would possibly let you." He blinked one eye, the other sparkling with mirth. "Well? I want to know what you think."

Before Darla could even start to formulate her thoughts about the changeable Cat Sidhe in front of her, he nudged the milkshake closer to her. "Oh. Yes."

She dipped a finger in—cold!—and sucked it between her teeth.

CHAPTER 8

Rory

ear fucking God, she was having a Harry Met Sally moment in a Greasy Spoon off the A90. Her face creased and her eyes unfocused, and she was sucking her finger. Sucking it.

No sooner had her finger touched her lips, Rory went rock hard, painfully pressing against the waistband of his jeans, *Let me at her, let me at her.*

He discreetly shifted his legs and adjusted himself, but she did not relent. She closed her eyes, her jaw going slack.

Then she moaned. *Moaned.* Loud enough that the server turned her head so sharply she nearly snapped some of her rigid platinum blonde ringlets.

"Can you…" Rory's voice was strained, hoarse. He dug his hands into his thighs, pinpricks of claws spearing through his arousal. "Keep it down," he whispered.

But oh, she would make that noise in bed too. The way she intently studied everything made Rory feel like the only man on the planet. Surely, she would want to explore some carnal delights; he could imagine her mapping his terrain like a diligent cartographer, noting every valley and peak of pleasure between them with that sense of wonder... Shit, man, she got excited about a crappy chocolate milkshake. An orgasm might blow her mind, literally, and in a very bad way.

But while she delved into what was clearly new experiences here for her, he had an inkling that she was not truly innocent of everything. Wherever she was from, she would have endured hardship and drudgery, just the same as anyone else. Looking into her face, he wondered if she brought the wonder into everything she did. A way of looking at the world and seeing it fresh, anew. Having that gaze turned on him, well. It revitalised Rory; something was recharging, responding, and not just his cock.

Calm down. She's probably a siren. Maybe a many tentacled monster, something from Lovecraft's wettest dream. Maybe she would eat him inside out and back to front.

Or maybe he would eat her out. Imagining her laying back, panting, her muscled legs tightening around his head, that look on her face, as if he were the only thing in the world...

Stop it. She's in need of help.

A flash of blue and red lights strobing his vision brought him down like a plunge in the cold North Sea. Fantasizing about banging her on the table would have to wait.

"Shit." Rory hunkered down lower. "The redcaps killed those humans to take their forms. I'm such a dumbass."

"Huh?" Her eyes slid open, languid, the pupils wider and a deep velvet black. They flinched back to small dots at the onslaught from the strobing police lights. "What are they?"

"Police, looking for those murdering redcaps, and I took the car with the evidence in it." Which meant even in the 1990's they could track down the vehicle numberplate.

"Fascinating," Darla said, slurping her milkshake.

Rory rolled his eyes. "No, not fascinating. Annoying, because our breakfast just got interrupted."

What to do, what to do. Option one, get arrested quietly, and disappear on the fuzz later. It had the advantage of not having to pay for the meal. Option two, assume that they would shoot first and ask questions later, and flee from them. If these police had any experience with redcaps, they wouldn't let one start a spoken sentence let alone a prison sentence. Rory and Darla would be filled with bullets before they took two steps out of the cafe. The thought of that filled his mouth with the taste of bile. No, trusting that they would be lenient wasn't an option.

Option three, then, was make a portal out of here. Rory flexed his hands. Exhaustion tugged at him, and he only had one small marble of magic left. "Back to the bathroom," he barked at Darla.

She tried to stand but buckled on her leg. Swinging her into his arms, Rory ran, hustling past the waitress whose eyes were fixed on the police presence outside, coffee overpouring into a mug and hissing on the floor.

Rory bundled the small and wriggling Darla into the storeroom. "Here goes nothing." Smashing the concentrated magic between his palms to help, he threw out his hands, trying to find the threads of reality sliding past him. One snagged on his claws, the tug of silk. Two! A miracle. Sinking his claws in, he set his shoulders. This was like tearing a boulder apart with his bare hands. He didn't know if he would be up to it, if the effort or even the attempt would drain his life. *But I have to try.* The idea of a bullet slamming into Darla's chest or her temple, a spray of blood and that light from her eyes fading...

Darla put her hand on his back.

Power, pure and simple, surged through Rory. He was unstoppable. *I can do this.* Never mind that Rory hadn't made a successful tear in the Veil that hadn't knocked him flat since the mid fifteenth century, *this time was it.* With a roar, Rory ripped through the Veil. Through immense luck he could see the Cat Sidhe's stolen castle, even the gardens, drenched in topaz light.

Rory stood stymied by his victory. "Holy shit, I did it!" Rory grinned at Darla.

A scream outside. "Police! Down on the floor!"

Rory grabbed Darla's hand in his shaking one. "I need you to answer me a question, truthfully. Does anything stop you from entering the fae realm? Were you disbarred, banned, is it death for you to enter?"

"Not to my knowledge," she said faintly, staring at the wavering rend in the world. Objectively it was spectacular, a blur of light rendered into rainbows stretching off inside this tear, and subjectively Rory was immensely proud of it. Something about her—her touch?—drove away Rory's exhaustion, both physical and mental.

He grinned. "Then let's go."

Her wide eyes turned to him. "Is this your home?"

"Yes."

She turned toward a crash from inside the restaurant and Rory grabbed her shoulders. "I'll make sure you get back here. Alright? Well, not here specifically, because this place is going to get noisy for a while." He fought the urge to shake her. "We have to go. Now! Trust me."

She nodded once, her face flushed. "I do."

Rory took a step forward and his stomach lurched as half of him existed in one plane and the other struggled to catch up. Tasting blood, Rory pushed through it, snatching Darla close to his chest. Wrapping his arms around her shoulders, he pulled her to him. If she felt too much of the dislocation she might panic and struggle against it.

The pain faded. Rory's senses unfurled with caution, and he opened his eyes. He was home, or at least in the gardens, and his stomach relaxed as the portal self-healed, sealing up behind them.

Darla tentatively lifted her head, and he watched her take the garden all in from within his arms. He had seen it all before, all the golden glory of the grasses, the roses that raced up the sides of the ruins, the greenhouses sheltering vegetables for the season, tenderly nurtured underneath cracked glass panes. Behind them slumped the castle, an edifice built long before the Cat and Cu Sidhe by some long extinct entity. It would have decayed had the Cat Sidhe not moved in one day, declaring it was theirs by dint of it being proportioned for them.

He watched for her reaction, how her pupils slowly expanded. She stared at the layout of the lawns and then up at the shadowed building around them. She was lost for words for once, and Rory smiled, proud to do that to her.

"Where are we?" she whispered.

Rory was loathe to release her to gesture, so he jerked his head to get her attention. "This part is the territory that the Cat Sidhe claim and maintain." He nodded toward the expanse of the horizon. The sun hung low in the sky; almost twilight.

Darla turned that inquisitive gaze to watch the sinking sun, her pupils widening in the dimmer topaz light, and Rory had never hated a stupid sunset more. He searched for something else to say, some other bait to get her to turn that gaze onto him again, but he found a sort of stillness, having her in his arms, watching her see this for the first time.

She settled against him, her body cooler than he expected. Refreshing. "I have never heard anything about this."

"No stories, no tales? I'm shocked you haven't at least heard of the Worldheart."

She took a deep breath, as if scenting the air. He relaxed his hold so she could breathe fully, but only a little.

"Ah! I can feel currents of it, coming from there." She wriggled a hand free and pointed directly toward a tower where the tether to the Worldheart was.

Like everything else the Cat Sidhe had claimed, the tower that held it was crumbling but stubbornly maintained, and the

Worldheart itself stroked against his soul sense, weak and watery where once it had been strong. "It's even worse than before."

"Worse?" Her eyes rounded and she folded her legs underneath her. "Why?"

Rory set his teeth. "We don't know exactly, but I believe it's because the Cu Sidhe are starving the Worldheart. Souls, the spirits of the departed, can be concentrated into magic using the right tools, but the Cu Sidhe are instead tossing them down their waterfall to the Otherworld. A true waste. Magic is depleted because they are shaving away at it, throwing away souls when we need them." Rory bit his tongue. He was getting passionate, reciting one of Orla's diatribes as if it would matter.

Darla tucked her hair behind her ear. "Has anyone tried talking to the Cu Sidhe about this?"

Rory snorted. "Cat and Cu Sidhe did all the talking they are ever going to do and each side has made their case plain and clear. There is no bridge between us; the impasse in ideology is a gulf. They are stubbornly insistent and so we do what we must. Millenia of war over the right to be the garbage men and women. But we are making treasure out of trash, while they are just throwing it away."

Rory stilled his hands. At some point, they had become animated. Since when did he pontificate like that? Treasure out of trash, what kind of Mad Men advertising hell did that get dredged from?

But Darla was entranced. All this beauty and glory in the gardens and she stared at him as though...

As though I matter.

She twisted a lock of hair in her fingers. "I haven't heard both sides... but I would want to be useful."

Rory's heart twinged. Of course, she would want to try and learn and grow, this situation and every twist and turn were a fascination to her. How many lifetimes would she need to live before that joy faded, to be replaced by an ennui that sucked at her spirit, dragging her down like chains.

He leaned away from her. She didn't deserve such dark thoughts. Let her have her fun.

She looked at him, concerned, and briefly Rory worried that he might have spoken, but then she reached out a hand. "I'm here," she said.

Rory pasted on a smile. "What's this for?"

She frowned as if doubting herself, then ploughed on. "You looked a bit lost. I'm telling you; we're here, in this place, together. We aren't lost. We know exactly where we are."

"I'm not lost, this is my back garden." Rory pointed. "Over there is the arbour where Kade and I used to sneak out; by here is the fountain we played in over the summers. The lands beyond are wonderful for game hunting." He gave her a flash of his lengthened canines.

She seemed pensive, sneaking glances at him. "How long would it take me to explore this place?"

"How long have you got?" he joked. "It depends how into it you get. You could spend centuries here, probably, and not get bored, not if chocolate milkshake sends you into paroxysms of delight."

She shrank in on herself. "I have seven days before I need to be back."

"Seven days? Why seven days? Do you turn into something else...? No, I won't pry," he said in response to her face clamming up. His chest warmed to see her flush as he teased her. "Well, there's lots to see here in the fae realm, and there aren't any humans, if those are what you're worried about."

If he had thought she was pleased by a milkshake before, it was nothing compared to the delight that suffused her face at his explanation. "No humans?"

Her smile sank claws deep in his heart. "Nope."

She lunged into his arms and pushed her face against his.

CHAPTER 9
Darla

Selkies expressed strong emotions through tangling their whiskers, the sensitive strands sending backwards and forwards a myriad of information. Emotions like joy, anger, or fear, and then sentiments, like sincere gratitude and happiness at seeing a familiar face. Darla's instinct was to tangle whiskers to share her pure happiness.

She could explore this world above the waters for untold centuries, and no time would pass for her sister! Where would she start? What would she do first? And all the while secure that her life waited for her at home, nothing to be missed, no family events to pine over, her whole life waiting for her to restart when she returned.

It was perfect.

After pressing her cheek to Rory's, she settled back onto her heels and clapped her hands. "What's first?"

Her heart fell when he remained stationary, as if mired in mudflats, staring at her.

"What?" She patted her cheeks. "Did I do something wrong?"

"I... no." He coughed. "Don't be too forward with other fae.

They might think that you mean something else by such close contact."

"Oh, a courtship thing?"

He leapt up, brushing off his trousers. "Yes. And then some." He held out a hand down for her, but Darla stood without it, unfolding from the ground. He took a step back, arms crossed over his chest. "You have to understand, we're a jaded lot. Immortality does something to fae, and boredom sends you down a few dark paths."

Unease crawled up her skin, the skin of this human form that she wore. Something about the change in Rory's demeanour sent chills through her. Was it this place? "Is this place dangerous?" she asked outright.

His eyes flashed. "Very. But I'll put the word about that you're my guest. In fact, let's get that clear straight away." Beckoning her, he walked briskly toward one of the larger buildings.

Stone. Marble. Darla knew these words and their water-buried states. Seawater ate and etched at even the hardest stone over time, leaving its own marker of the effect of the passage of time. To see it freshly cut with edges so sharp she felt they might cut her palm if she touched them! Their steps rang out crisply, echoing around the room.

And more people! Darla's smile stretched from ear to ear to see more examples of the humanoid form. Some with short hair, others with tumbling ringlets; some wearing huge, bulbous dresses that made them look like a furled anemone, others wearing strips of material that writhed around their limbs like tentacles looking for a passing meal. They peered at her as though scenting something in the air, something new and delicious.

She waved to them all, a jaunty flip that signalled her intent to remain friendly, and bared her teeth, to show that she was not unarmed, just in case.

Rory was stiff and tense beside her, nodding to the guard

who let them pass unmolested. Rory's relaxed familiarity in the restaurant was gone now. *I wish I had been able to take that picture of him like that.* Still, she could call it to mind. Darla hardly ever forgot details when she memorised them. Hopefully there would be more opportunities for them to relax, and maybe this realm wasn't so good if she had to be on her guard all the time.

Rory drew closer to her, warmth brushing against her side. "This is the inner court of our queen, the Cat Sidhe ruler Orla. She's my older sister."

"I see." In the commune, blood ties were prized and protected. "Are you close?"

"Close in that she was raised by our parents, and Kade and I were raised by the wet nurse."

"How old are you exactly?"

His ears flushed. "Never mind. We're here now, Queen Orla's office. She'll likely be in here, and I'm minded to wait with my boots muddying the desk if she's not."

Unsure how to take that, Darla let the information sit between them and waited to see how it would develop. Rory knocked his knuckles hard against the wood in a loud rap, and a voice called, "There you are, Ruairí."

Behind the thick door was a library, whole rows of books ordered neatly like a seaweed farm. Seated at the work-worn table was a woman with a pile of red ringlets gathered at the nape of her neck and a glowing rectangle of light suspended in front of her face. It was the first overt use of magic Darla had seen apart from the portals, and she gasped.

The woman looked up at Rory with a warm smile on her bronzed face, the smile turning to Darla to bathe her in the same glow.

I hope I smile at Neri like that. The stray thought tugged at Darla.

"Ruairí, I see you have returned. And in record time." Stoppering her pen and dismissing the light with a wave of her fingers, the woman stood up. She had an enviable control of her slim limbs as she sauntered around the table and offered Darla her hand, palm down.

Darla made an appreciative hum. "I love your wrists. Very nice."

Rory stifled a snort. "You are supposed to plant a kiss on the back of her hand. Though I'm not sure I would; you can never tell how dirty Orla's hands are."

A flash of annoyance crossed Orla's face, quickly replaced with that beatific sisterly smile. "A warm welcome to you, traveller. You do not have to place your lips on my skin; rubbing your whiskers along it will do."

Darla's throat tightened. How did this fae know she usually sported whiskers? Perhaps she thought her a Cat Sidhe like herself.

Her offer constituted a one-way information transfer. That did not seem fair to Darla, that this woman would know Darla's state and not disclose her own. However, it was only likely she could sense her excitement and trepidation, the usual dual edge of visiting a new place. After a hasty rub of her cheeks against the back of her hand, Darla straightened up.

Orla turned her attention to Rory. "What can I do for you, aside from the usual after a foray in the human worlds? Food and drink have already been sent up to your rooms."

Rory was scanning the bookshelves like he couldn't care less. What was with him all of a sudden? In a bored tone he said, "I'll tell all later, of course, but for now, I want protections extended around my guest here."

"Mm. Granted, of course. You can have your pick of the guest rooms, my dear. I'll let the servants know to put them under the name...?"

"Don't," Rory snapped before Darla could even open her mouth. "She's my guest. That's the end of it."

Darla recalled their conversation about true names. "I don't want to be walking around being called Rory's guest."

He scowled as if annoyed at her interruption. "Why not? My name will ensure a great deal of people know not to bother or hinder you." He tossed up a hand. "Use it, abuse it, or not as you see fit."

Was he only pretending that he didn't care? Perhaps he did not. They had only met mere hours before, after all, and in that time shared true names and fought beside one another. What did this change in demeanor mean?

Darla's gaze slid to Orla, who in turn was locked in a staring match with Rory. The queen smirked and broke it off to address Darla. "As annoying as my little brother is when he's right, even I have to admit that this is the more sensible course of action. Do be careful with your true name, little one. I would not have used it for ill against you, but many might." She sighed. "Fae have so little occupation these days that mischief and mayhem are all that they aspire to."

"Seems a waste of lifetimes," Darla said.

"It is," Orla murmured. "It is. But for now, we have more pressing concerns. Rory, I will call up a servant to show your esteemed guest to her rooms and arrange some suitable company, and we will have that little debrief." She pulled on a fabric cord.

"I look forward to it," Rory grunted, looking up and down the spines of the books.

Darla went to his side. "What are you looking for?"

He stepped smartly aside as if moving out of her way. Or maybe to get away from her. "Merely passing the time until that servant arrives."

Darla took a tentative step back. Perhaps she was too close to him and he didn't like it.

The door rapped and male fae entered. "Your Majesty? What is it you require?" He was so tall his head brushed the ceiling, and his arms were as big around as Darla's waist. One side of his face had a silver mask that fitted to his face; the other had a mass of scars. His white eyeball stared at Rory in particular.

"Wow. You have very big muscles," Darla said.

The new man shifted his stance with an ominous creak of is leathers.

Orla chuckled. "Kater, please take our newest honoured guest to a suite. She might want to bathe and change into something a bit more setting appropriate. Please find her a suitable companion to occupy her time and help her make the most of her stay here in this realm. Oh, and do remind everyone that she is Ruairí's."

The man bowed low, leathers creaking even more. "Of course, Your Majesty."

She had been handed off? "I don't belong to anyone," she said, annoyed.

Rory smirked. "Just use it to your advantage. You'll get used to the privilege it affords you, I'm sure."

He was different again, from stiff and tense to overly relaxed. What was his true nature? Where was the joking fae from the diner, he had seemed true to himself then as he explained his perception of the world?

Confused at his change of heart, Darla followed the servant out. She had studied trees that had fallen into the sea and been stripped bare by the current, turning into hardened but pale trunks, and this servant gave her a feeling like that, as if life had whittled him to the core and what was left was an impassive calm. He probably had a wealth of wisdom to share, if she could get him talking.

He walked beside her, matching his steps to hers. "Are you well, miss? It seems as though you are limping."

"Oh. Yes. A run in with some redcaps." She grinned. "I gave as good as I got, I think."

He nodded gravely. "The queen instructed that I take you to your rooms directly. I can send up a healer immediately after I get you settled."

Leading her down the echoing corridor and up some stairs, Kater let her proceed him. Darla laid her hand on the marble balustrade. It was cold, even to her. "Have you been here long?"

He cocked his head. "Time means nothing here, miss, but if you mean how much time has passed in the human realm, then only seven centuries, miss. I know enough about the castle and surroundings to provide you with correct directions, should you require them."

Seven centuries? Darla gulped. The blocks of stone were weathered and rounded, pieces of greenery finding a toe hold and establishing themselves. "I didn't realise castles had plants in them."

Kater plucked out a particularly pretty trailing plant with a riot of yellow flowers, tearing its roots from the walls. "They typically do not, miss. The Cat Sidhe have only recently acquired it; those aforementioned seven centuries or so. It requires significant maintenance, rather like the realm itself."

Darla felt sorry for the plant in Kater's hands. There were plenty of others, however, all firmly establishing themselves as a kind of living tapestry on the walls. It reminded Darla very much of the seabed and caves that her colony called home.

"So, you didn't build it? Who did?"

"No one is sure of that answer, miss, although pundits are always keen to provide their theories as fact."

"How big is it?"

"Big enough to comfortably house the royal family: Orla, Rory and Kade. A throne room, which has had most of the structural modifications. It would not do to have those collapse on esteemed guests. Those corridors there,"—he waved back the way they had come—"have an administrative function, with many offices and meeting rooms. These up here are the living quarters; guests on this floor, and then the royal family's chambers further along."

He didn't ask any questions. *Is he not curious, or does he feel he cannot?*

"You can ask questions of me, if you like," she offered.

He flexed his hands. "Not at this time, miss." He gestured to a door. "We are here."

Entering through a large wooden door, Darla was immediately impressed with the space. A bed took up the left-hand side, and to the right, a series of panels in the same thick wood. There were no plants here, only soft fabrics laid on the floor and draped on the comfortable looking chair. Touching the panels, Darla found they opened to an enormous selection of clothes. "These are lovely fabrics. So, this is how dresses look."

Kater extended one hand. "If I may suggest, the yellow would suit you, miss."

"You think?" She rubbed the silk against her cheek. It vibrated with an impression, a memory indelibly laid into the fabric.

It was of a man's bare chest pressed against it, sweat streaking his skin, sliding his hands underneath the fabric...

Darla came back to herself. Kater gently uncurled his hands from her upper arms. He had steered her away from the dress. "You are especially sensitive to the enhancements, I see."

Darla wiped her forehead with a shaking hand. Her body trembled, her core a wavering warmth. "What was that?"

He waved his hand at the clothes. "These will have standard enhancements on them to increase their effectiveness. Many fae have a natural defence against charms and the like. These are for amusement, and to signal one's intent strongly."

Darla sucked in air between her teeth. "So, if I was to wear that dress outside..."

He bowed his head. "It would send up an impression like a scent for a cat in heat. It seems, though, that you have no defence against the enhancements yourself. I will arrange for more specific clothes to be made for you."

Unspoken was the question every fae seemed to have: what are you? Darla turned away so she wouldn't have to confront it. "Thank you. I'd appreciate it." Still, how that dress had made her feel...

She had memorised Rory's bare chest when he had torn his shirt to pieces to stem the bleeding in her leg. What would he feel like to touch? His hands were warm and he had pressed her against him less than an hour ago to transport them here, her cheeks and the remnants of her whiskers close against his neck. It had been a warm and intimate place, the beat of his heart trembling under her senses.

"Ahem." Kater cleared his throat again, waiting for something.

"Oh. Sorry. It's been a long day." Crawling out of the sea this morning, would she ever have imagined going to a new realm entirely? *As long as you come back*, a voice that sounded like her sister whispered in her mind, a thread of fear shooting through her. *I will.* Rory had said he would bring her back, and in plenty of time. *I can spend as long as I want here, exploring.* Darla was in control of this little jaunt.

Kater cleared his throat as she stood there daydreaming again. "If there's nothing else, I will leave you now to freshen up. I will send a healer, who might also be a suitable companion for miss. I have not been given specific instruction regarding your evening, so unless master Rory orders differently, I am contented to either arrange for your attendance at dinner or have something sent up."

Master Rory? "We will see," Darla said, uncertainty colouring her excitement but not dampening it. "I don't know that I'll be able to rest, but I know I should." It would be sensible, and she had all the time in the world to explore to her heart's content. The realm wasn't going anywhere.

Except it was. Magic was seeping out of the land.

Darla held up a hand. "If it's not too much trouble, I'd like to... learn more about the magic problem."

Kater showed the first visible sign of being wrong-footed, his eye widening, but he quickly recovered. "A most commendable topic of inquiry. I am more content in my choice of companion; Rhiannon is well versed and familiar with the library and can assist you."

Darla twisted her fingers together. "Thank you."

"You are more than welcome." Clicking his heels together, he made his way to the door. "Do not hesitate to call on me if you require anything. I am delighted to make your acquaintance, miss."

"And I, yours." Darla waved as he left, closing the door behind him.

Darla sank into the bed but then quickly jumped up to explore. There was so much to see in here alone, and even another heavy wooden door. This opened to reveal a tiled room given over to an enormous basin. Taps let water tumble into the chipped tub, and Darla wriggled out of her jeans to inspect her injury. The wrap Rory had made still held, and she smoothed it, evidence of his care. She hadn't imagined it, he had been attracted to her! But why hide it from his own sister?

The door rapped. "Hello! Rhiannon here."

Darla opened the door and a short fae with shifting colours in her short hair and a warm smile entered. "May I come in? Kater says you have an injury, and I've brought emeralds to help with that."

Emeralds? How did those help with injury? Darla would normally ask, but a wave of shyness crept over her as the new fae set out her bag on the desk, pulling out a gemstone with a faint green glow at its heart. How many new people had she met today? Were all of them Cat Sidhe?

Rhiannon gently asked, "Is it all a bit much? I can see to your leg quietly and then leave you to rest."

Rubbing her eyes, Darla shook her head. "It's been a long day, and a lot has happened. I'm sorry to be so rude, I usually have uncountable questions, but right now I'm so tired I can't think." Darla slumped in her seat.

"That's alright," Rhiannon soothed, snapping shut her case. "Here's an emerald. Can you heal yourself using it?"

"Only by the hand that hurts me," she repeated, taking the stone Rhiannon offered. Immediately the green heart inside it flared, a bright glare stinging Darla's eyes. She blinked the tears back, dropping the stone.

Rhiannon stood stunned, then galvanised into action, picking up the stone and holding it near Darla's leg. Underneath the bandage, the pain eased.

"Wow." Rhiannon held the now vibrant stone, the green reflecting in her eyes. "I... I'll go now. But... wow." She went without another word, leaving Darla alone in this new world.

Darla made it to the bed, where the yellow dress lay out alongside Rory's jacket. She fingered the collar and then rested her head on it. It smelled like him, and touching the dress made those images well up again, of his warm arms pressing her close to a fiercely beating heart. Her own feelings surged up in response, the reaction in her body immediate.

Sweet dreams indeed. What a great first day! Darla sank into a victorious sleep.

CHAPTER 10

Rory

The times when Rory would tell Orla exactly how he felt were measured in centuries past, not just decades. Bringing Darla here to make sure she had the full protection of the crown placed upon her was necessary, but that didn't mean that Rory wanted to air his half-formed feelings in front of his scheming sister.

Still, he couldn't help but stretch his senses toward Darla. Kater would ensure her complete safety, but he was Orla's slave through and through. Darla was a powerful glow, someone anyone in this realm could sense. Shit, had he just brought the equivalent of a beacon pointing straight at them for the Cu Sidhe to want to find?

Orla poured two glasses of the deep burgundy wine she favoured for special occasions. "Ruairí, sit."

Rory perched his backside on the edge of her workstation instead. If he had had his tail in this form, he would have swept it over the desk just to send papers scattering. Keeping Orla's attention away from Darla would be his priority, and if that meant annoying her even more than usual, then so be it.

Orla passed him a crystal wine glass without comment. "Well?" she asked softly.

Rory took it by the stem, swirling so the liquid tidal-waved against the confines of the glass. "What do you want me to say? I failed. I'm terribly sorry for the waste of magic used to get me there, and I'm drained dry for the foreseeable." He gulped down half the measure in his glass and smacked his lips. "Ahh. No souls today, I'm afraid."

Orla looked him up and down, setting her glass to a small side table. Then she put a hand to her face, a smile spreading behind it. "Oh, don't tell me. You don't know?"

"Don't know what?" Rory scowled. "What, has the crisis been alleviated since I was gone?" A beat of hope shot through his center that Rory squashed. It wouldn't ever be that simple.

But Orla's eyes were bright, as if she had secured victory. "It is now. Ruairí, you are to be congratulated, and I cannot believe you don't realise. Surely this is a prank, you have to know!"

Claws slid out of Rory's fingers with a spike of pain. "Know *what*, sister dear? Recall that I don't like jokes unless I'm the one behind them."

Orla screamed with laughter. "You really don't know! How precious." Leaning forward, face splitting with a smile Rory hadn't seen for decades, as if all her cares had been lifted and his sister had returned at last, she clasped his knee. "You've brought us a selkie."

The stem of the glass snapped in Rory's sudden fist. *Shit.* A selkie. *A selkie?*

Jagged glass poked at him. Rory cleared his throat, cupping the bowl of the wine glass. "Selkies are extinct."

"Yes, they were supposed to be." Orla pressed her hands together in front of her chest. "Ruairí, her very being is made of a collection of souls, not just one. She is a powerhouse of raw potential. Surely, you must have felt it?"

The way Darla's touch had meant he could tear all the way

through reality into his own realm, and how her focused attention had reawoken something within him to respond in turn. His heart jerked painfully. How she made him feel... was how she made everyone feel.

"Ruairí, with the energy in her skin alone, Sèitheach is beaten for sure." Orla's claws slid out, kneading the arms of the chair she sat in. "Meanwhile her very presence will energise everybody. Look at you, I haven't seen you glowing like this since... well. Fifteenth century, at least."

Rory's throat hurt. "What do you mean, her skin?"

Orla waved a hand. "Oh, her pelt. Selkies shed their forms to appear human. Do you have it?"

Rory's heart beat fast. Very fast. Those souls he had sensed, that had been Darla herself, Darla leaving the ocean and peeling off her pelt.

Orla tipped her head. "What's wrong? This is an amazing coup, Ruairí, I'm so proud of you. I thought you'd be boasting up and down by now."

He forced a smile onto his face. What had he done, bringing Darla here? "What do we do now?"

Orla clapped her hands. "Show me the pelt; I cannot wait to see it!"

Rory shook his head once, dry mouthed.

"Ah. Unfortunate, but you can go and retrieve it. The power in it will sustain our realm for decades, Ruairí. Do you know what this means?" Orla was invigorated, finally on the cusp of winning the war for the Cat Sidhe and taking the Topaz Court for themselves.

"She... I mean, it's hers. Her pelt." Take Darla's skin? Keep it from her? His own skin was inseparable from him, so he couldn't begin to imagine peeling it off and discarding it, but it was *hers*. "It's part of her."

"Exactly. Ruairí, we are talking about our survival. If we used the pelt to sustain the realm, we would no longer need to sneak and steal a soul here and a soul there, always a fraught mission risking the lives of our bravest Cat Sidhe and costly when they fail. It will also give me all the power I need to challenge Sèitheach and win. This is it, Ruairí, this is the balance about to be restored!"

"Yes. I... Yes." Rory's throat closed.

Orla cocked her head, a small smile flickering on the edges of her lips. "Why, little brother. How you hesitate at this when previous missions risked your life and more." She rang a finger around the rim of the glass, the haunting note causing goosebumps to prickle his arms.

Orla's dark eyes watched him. "You can ask me what you want to ask. I promise I won't read anything into it." She winked at him.

He clenched his fists. Orla always had to win. "What will happen to her?" he growled.

Orla's smug smile was rich and warm with satisfaction. "Why, nothing." She perched on the desk next to him, taking his hand in hers, wincing at the glass in his palm. As she picked it out, she spoke in a low voice. "While she visits us, her pelt is better off here, rather than in the human realm for anyone to stumble across. The pelt will be unchanged through our use. Energy can be neither created nor destroyed, but this is a lot of energy, Ruairí. Hardly anything she would miss, and she herself, why, she seems perfectly gregarious. Her presence among the Cat Sidhe will restore a lot of spirits. We won't even need to draw on magic whilst she is here, we will make her the toast of the nation and she will adore all the attention." Putting the glass shards aside, Orla studied the back of her hand. "She will turn the tide for us, Ruairí." Waving her hand over Rory's, his skin came together and knitted smoothly.

A profligate use of power. Would she have done that if Rory hadn't succeeded as much as he had? Bile burned the back of his throat. Her insidious logic sang like a siren song.

Orla stroked the back of his hand like a caring older sister. "You will not need to risk lives in the attempt to gather enough souls to keep us—the land—going. We can rest, regroup, and finally plan to get ahead of those dogs, and start to make some real change. She is very, very powerful. We cannot let this opportunity slide by and slip away back under the waves." Placing her hands either side of his head, Orla leaned in. "Ruairí, we cannot let this go."

The tiredness sank into his very bones. *I cannot keep doing this.* Especially now that he felt what it could be like, with her. Was this Orla's doing, manipulating him?

He threw Orla's hands off. "We cannot let *her* go, you mean."

She smiled. "Precisely." She rolled her eyes. "Don't get all noble Kade on me, Rory, you were always the more practical one. And besides, you can show her the time of her life. Why would she ever want to go back?"

Darla had to have come from somewhere, there were probably others like her. He kept his lips sealed about that inkling.

Orla drummed her fingers on the stem of her wine glass. "Ruairí, think carefully about what I've said. What options do I have in front of me to choose from?"

Rory closed his eyes. Option one, she could let the land die, but that wasn't an option she could or would countenance and made him feel sick. Option two, she could use the selkie's power. If it didn't hurt her, what therefore was the harm? That still twisted his insides just as badly as the first.

"We could ask her," he said.

Orla turned sideways to look at him. "She might say no. Then what would our options be?"

Rory's stomach twisted even further. He shook his head. Orla meant to keep Darla here, willing or not.

Orla put her hands flat on the table. "This is all beside the point. She seemed eager to stay here for a time, enthusiastic.

Once the fight with Shay is over and I am the victor, the balance will be restored. No more sending the souls of the dead into the Otherworld. Then, of course, she will be free to come and go as she pleases, none the wiser that there was ever any need for her to stay in luxury for a short time. And we are doing it for good, Ruairí. We are doing what is right, what is necessary. When has a few weeks in paradise ever been a hardship?"

She smiled at Rory, tucking his hair behind his ear with sisterly concern. "This might be the saving of you as well. I meant it when I said you seem to be revitalised. Now, you can't keep her all to yourself, you know." Orla winked. "I will have Rhiannon take her around tomorrow. You will see the impact she has on the other Cat Sidhe, on our people. She will do our vulnerable good." Orla danced her fingertips on the desk, claws clicking. "And then you'll want to secure her pelt."

Rory held his arms tightly against his chest, holding himself together.

Orla leaned back in her chair. "I don't want to have to make that an order, Ruairí. Rest for a time, come to me for more magic, and then you will retrieve the pelt. Take Kater with you; he will be able to assist should anything unexpected crop up."

Like me deciding not to go through with it. "Of course, Orla." His back was against the wall, but his sister meant only the best for the realm. Was it really too much to ask of a selkie to stay, when the alternative was so dire?

Orla smiled. "Good, Ruairí. Good. Now, that's all for tonight."

Rory bowed and saw himself out, looking back at Orla as he closed the door to her study.

Her topaz eyes glinted in the harsh blue light as she fired up her viewer. Her face was smooth, shoulders pushed back, but her arm shook ever so slightly.

CHAPTER 11
Darla

arla's whiskers sent conflicting messages. Her sister should have been nearby, and her warm bulk was missing. Moreover, everything smelled different. But she also sensed safety and security. Everything was as it was before she went to sleep, which was impossible, because...

Sitting up, Darla disturbed the silk sheets, and they slid to pool around her limbs. Her human limbs. Had she really only left the sea yesterday? So much had happened, from leaving her sister and her pelt behind, to running into Rory...

A rhythmic noise outside dragged her attention from thinking of the enigmatic fae. She scrambled to the window, dislodging the dress and jacket and shoving her curls away from her forehead.

There! *A horse!* She had heard tales of these creatures, with more legs than a car. She clutched her hands in front of her chest, then let out a loud bark and waved wildly.

The man seated on the horse darted his head up, then waved back with jerky movements.

The door knocked, with Rhiannon's soft voice calling, "Are you awake yet, Darla?"

"I am! And I've seen a horse!" Darla cried. Barking from the window alerted her. She turned back around. "Oh! And a dog!"

Rhiannon came in, her eyes widening as she took Darla in, then burst out laughing. "Oh my! You've given the postman an eyeful."

Darla looked down at her naked body. "Oh. I forgot that humans like coverings. Fae do as well, I take it?"

Rhiannon slid the wardrobe doors wide. "What's your fancy today? You've got a good, solid selection here; Kater knows what suits a woman."

Darla wrapped her arms around her midsection. "I liked the clothes I had on yesterday."

"Jeans and a crop top, got it." Rhiannon slung her a black pair of the thick cloth they called jeans and a short top with words on it.

"Look, but don't touch," Darla read aloud.

"Yes." Rhiannon winked. "It's a protection top, yes? It's got a small charm on it. If anyone touches it, an alert will go straight to Kater." Rhiannon grinned. "I can tune it to ping Rory if you like."

Darla pulled the top over her head to settle it over her shoulders, pulling it partway down her midsection, where the material ended. She pulled the jean tubes on one at a time, considering. "What is Rory doing today?"

"He's busy, so I'm assigned as your companion. That doesn't mean I'm not excited about the prospect, though! I love nothing better than trawling our markets and hiking to the edge of our lands."

A swell of cold lapped at Darla's stomach. Rory was too busy for her? Of course, he had his real life to attend to, he couldn't drop it just because she had sneaked out from the sea to explore.

Darla had to make the most of her time. "Yes, to all of these. Shall we go now?"

"Sure." Rhiannon pointed her toward the door. "Let's start with breakfast. I know a great place we can get something special! Oh, grab a coat. We have a saying here: If you don't like the weather, wait five minutes; it'll change."

Darla ran her hands over the myriad coats in the closet, her hands lingering over furs and leathers and cloth. Then she picked up Rory's red jacket. It smelled of herself and of him, somehow comforting and lending her extra bravery in this new place. "Coming."

Outside the tumbledown castle, Darla shaded her eyes. Over to the east was a deep, dense forest, with golds, bright oranges, and fiery reds winking in the sunlight. To the west crashed the sea, and Darla was curious about the mysteries in its depths here in the fae realm; would they be wildly different to those in the human realm?

She squinted up at the sun. "How long did I sleep?"

"You were very tired, you needed it."

"But I have so much I want to do! I don't want to sleep my time away!" Darla huffed.

Rhiannon gave her an odd look. "You know, time moves differently here."

"Oh, yes, Rory did say." Mentioning his name caused a swirl of strange emotions to stir up in Darla, muddying her feelings. Was that causality, or coincidence? She would have to think about those later; for now, there was too much to see.

Rhiannon led her to the market stalls, set out in long rows and attracting a crowd to jostle shoulder to shoulder. All manner of things were sold from clothes to chickens, and Darla stared slack-jawed as things she had only read about in water-logged books passed before her. Spices, heady and competing with each other so that her nose was overwhelmed. Intricately woven baskets. Jewellery set with stones glittering with prisms of rainbow light in their depths.

"That's pretty," Rhiannon cooed. "You should get it."

"What do I exchange for it?" Selkies used a currency, but what would the fae use? Promises, perhaps?

"Oh, I have money. Here." Rhiannon paid, and Darla selected a necklace with a tree design. "Lovely! That's a map of the Worldheart."

"Worldheart?"

"Yes, the river that runs from the highest reaches of the fae realm," she touched the silver tips of the delicate branches, "to the waterfall out of the realm and on the Otherworld." She tapped the base of the trunk. "No one knows what the Otherworld is like. Only souls of the dead go there, and no one has ever come back."

Darla's chest swelled with the new knowledge. Adventure truly waited around every corner! "If this river runs through the realm, where are we along it?"

"We're about here, I think." Her brightly painted fingernail hovered on one of the thicker branches near an offshoot.

How interesting. Selkies communicated knowledge on where places were in relation to other landmarks through songs, and here was as physical representation. She put it around her neck and smiled at her new friend. "What's next?"

Darla was not used to so much warmth, neither in the air around her or the welcome from the citizens. Selkies were not creatures that ignored the different harems coldly, but they prized family and blood before all else. To be welcomed as if she were blood kin by merchants and people in the street was a special treat.

A table set out to the side attracted her notice. On it was curled up a small fluffy animal.

Darla jiggled Rhiannon's arm. "What's that?"

She looked over. "A plain cat, not a Cat Sidhe. See if it will say hi."

Darla placed her head close to the cat. It twitched an ear,

then its eyes slid open. It yawned widely in her face, not fazed by having another creature so close.

"It's beautiful," Darla said.

The cat twisted and turned its belly up into the air. The white fur was as soft as any seal pup fluff. "Ohhh. What a gift!" Darla crooned. The cat made a rumbling noise, vibrations rattling her fingertips. She smiled widely. "I like cats!"

Rhiannon laughed. "Good! Because the Cat Sidhe are cats, silly. But what are you? I haven't a clue."

Darla looked away. "I cannot say. Sorry." She felt bad, keeping something a secret when one's origins were so obviously flaunted in this realm. Perhaps the selkie matriarch had only been concerned about *humans* learning about selkies, though. Darla wished she could consult the matriarch. *For so long I wanted to be free from strictures, and here I am, placing them upon myself!*

Rhiannon's smile faltered. "You've got such a bright energy around you. I'd say you were a flower fae." She squeezed Darla's hand. "Is that why you keep saying you only have a few days?" she asked quietly.

Darla's eyes widened. "Oh, I'm not... Do flower fae only last a few days?" The poor things.

Rhiannon touched Darla's hair. "Well, I'm glad of that, at least." She cocked her head, green eyes twinkling. "You smell of the sea. Are you a siren?"

Darla felt her cheeks heat. "Why does everyone assume that? They aren't the only things in the sea, you know."

Rhiannon covered her mouth with her hand. Why? To hide her smile? Darla pulled the woman's hand down, then wondered if that was an aggressive move.

Fortunately, Rhiannon just laughed. "Sorry, I do that when I don't want to show my teeth accidentally. That can be taken as a warning to some fae."

Selkies too. So, customs were sometimes not that different, even across creatures. "Fascinating."

Rhiannon slid her arm around Darla's, and the close presence was welcome. Neri had always swum and curled up close to Darla; she was used to someone always at her side. Rhiannon pursed her lips. "So, my not-a-siren. Let's see if I can deduce what you are. Do you live in the sea?"

Not quite comfortable with the game but unsure how to proceed, Darla replied, "Mostly."

Rhiannon's eyes sparkled. "Ever lured a man to his doom?"

Darla huffed. "I'm *not* a siren! I don't recall having ever lured a single man, or woman for that matter, to drown in the depths." She tossed her hair. "That doesn't mean I haven't, by accident, of course. It's their fault if they can't control themselves."

"Absolutely." Rhiannon smiled widely. "I couldn't agree more."

A large tree grew in the centre of the marketplace. A great deal of stall holders used it in some way, hanging their wares on the lower branches, leaning blackboards against it to advertise the price, and even one enterprising mother using it as a swing for her child, pushing him while she tended to a customer's order.

Darla craned her head back to fully take it in, each swish of the branches and rustle of leaves. She had always imagined a tree would be like some of the large branching kelp, and to some extent there were similarities; how the extremities moved in the currents, whether water or air, waving back and forth. The tree was much more static, more immovable in its stance, like a statue. Another difference was that while the kelp originated from many different places to become a whole, this tree had only one large strong trunk from which life flowed up toward each individual leaf.

It all grows from one place, one root, one trunk.

"Darla!" Rhiannon took her hand to lead her on, setting aside her guessing game. There was a stone dragon further on, making a bridge over the thoroughfare. Darla marvelled at each individual scale as they passed underneath it. Surely it had to have been a real dragon to be so detailed?

"What's the hurry?" she asked Rhiannon.

"Only this!" The Cat Sidhe pointed to what looked like a set of three brown cylinders. Upon closer inspection, Darla realized it was actually a cascade of liquid the shade of turned over earth.

"What is that?" she asked, sniffing, before her senses suddenly alerted her.

Rhiannon leaned in close, her breath tickling Darla's ear. "It's something called a chocolate fountain."

Darla leaned in close while Rhiannon paid the stallholder. Darla lifted the fruit that she had been given and dippedit into the pond of chocolate underneath the fountain. The fruit resisted being pushed in, but the chocolate immediately clung to it, like an anemone wrapping around a morsel. Before too long, the bright red fruit was hidden underneath the chocolate.

"Oh dear." Rhiannon helped her to rescue it. "Now, close your eyes and take a bite."

Darla obeyed, opening her mouth wide. There was a beat of time where nothing happened; sounds of steps and people talking ebbed and flowed in the crowded marketplace, her whiskers utterly useless with so much movement swirling around her.

Just as she was about to open her eyes, the tip of the chocolate-covered delicacy touched her lip. Her tongue darted out to taste it: warm, yes, and rich, something slightly nutty, sweet— very sweet! Rhiannon eased it in, and Darla chomped down happily.

"That was..." Darla opened her eyes and made a noise

rather like she imagined a startled owl would make, and Rhiannon put her hands over her mouth to hide her smile.

"I'm so happy I took this journey. There's so much to see here!" She waved around herself with a laugh. "I don't know how I'll see it all in six days."

"Well." Rhiannon winked. "Don't tempt me. Fae have been known to trap people here for longer. Usually with more than chocolate, though."

"Chocolate would do it for me!" Darla said fervently.

They made their way out of the markets and the shadow of the castle, toward quieter streets. The paths weaved and wended in ways that Darla couldn't see the logic of, wishing she had some ability swim up and view it from above to see the size and what design drove it.

"This way," Rhiannon said, tugging Darla's wrist. "There's someone I want you to meet."

A newcomer, dressed in a gown overflowing with frills and gussets that made her look like a sea slug with fronds, waited in the quieter streets outside the market. Her red curls were pressed tightly to her head pulling her eyebrows up and back, giving her fish-belly-white face a rather startled expression.

Rhiannon stopped pulling at her and bowed low to the woman. "My good Lady Morag."

The woman extended a long-nailed hand toward Darla. Darla very much did not want this woman to touch her and backed away, an unpleasant tingle zapped across Darla's whiskers; she swallowed a yelp.

The woman sneered. "You're late."

"Late? Late for what?" A tiny twinge touched Darla's nerves. "I thought I had all the time in the universe? Who will mind if we *are* late? Where are we supposed to be?" Cat Sidhe hierarchies and family units had yet to be revealed to her, but while this was interesting information, it turned her stomach to see the friendly Rhiannon being dismissed by some higher-type figure. *If I refuse her, will this cause an uncomfortable situation for Rhiannon? Or help her?*

"The queen wanted you to meet the important people, not play in the market." The woman flicked her hand toward Darla. "Come here, girl. First you will visit my mother, who is very ill."

Darla had been about to make an excuse, any excuse, perhaps about going back to the castle, until the lady mentioned her mother. "She is ill? Hurt?" Darla frowned. "Did I accidentally hurt her?" Putting a hand over her mouth, Darla tried to recall any incident in the market. Had she knocked someone over and not been aware?

Lady Morag's face turned even more wrinkled as she pursed her lips and frowned. "Will that get you to come faster?"

"Take me to her." As they walked back along the street, Darla pressed her palms together. Selkies could be healed faster if they were helped by the hand that hurt them, if peace was made sincerely. Perhaps Cat Sidhe were the same!

The lady puffed and panted, waving Darla toward a row of very tall thin buildings, the spires surely high enough to stroke the sky. "Not so fast! I'm not as spry as you." She grabbed Darla's elbow and gasped. "Oh!"

Whirling to face her, Darla supported her arms as the woman reeled. The woman's eyes rolled, her fingers digging into Darla's elbows. Darla winced but held on as the lady sagged in her arms.

"My lady?" Rhiannon stepped closer, hesitantly.

"I'm fine! Fine. More than fine." Her head lifted, and Darla startled. Her skin, pasty white before, now gleamed with a light covering of pearlescent fur. Her eyes shone with an inner glow.

"Oh! My." Lady Morag put her hand to her face. "Oh, you wonderful thing! I feel at least a century younger."

Rhiannon rushed to Darla's side. "Are you alright?"

"I... yes? What happened, is this a Cat Sidhe thing?" Darla leaned in, fascinated. "You have lovely soft fur."

"Yes, it's very soft, dear, or at least it was when I was younger." A deep, rich sound came from her throat, like the cat's purr but deeper. Darker. "You will come with me. You will have whatever you wish, toys, clothes, whatever food your kind eats. You—"

"My kind?" Fear wrapped around Darla's throat. "I... I'm not sure what you mean."

"A selkie, the first selkie in centuries." Lady Morag licked her lips.

It was as if an unexpected wave had slammed into her, turning her over and around with no indication of which way was up. *She knows what I am.* What would happen now? The matriarch had been afraid of this very situation.

"I... I have to go. I want to go." Darla wished she could swim up and away. *Am I about to learn why selkies should remain hidden?* What consequences would visit the colony because of her actions?

"Lady Morag?" a woman called, approaching in a flourish of skirts, a tall man trailing behind her. "Why, you look very restored!" She grabbed the lady's shoulders. "Have you been granted some magic? Where from? Who has it?"

"Yes, Morag, you must share!" The man glared sternly at Darla. "Are you giving out the magic?"

"Who's giving out magic?" Another lady came close, hands grasping her skirts.

"We have to go," Rhiannon hissed. Darla tore her hands from Lady Morag, and a scream rose up after them as Rhiannon grabbed Darla's arm. "Run, Darla! Run now!"

They sprinted down the twisty streets, the shining buildings flashing in Darla's vision, when a huge cat dropped down in Rhiannon's path.

Rhiannon snarled at them, claws lengthening. "Get back behind me, Darla!"

"I can fight!" Darla bared her teeth at the cat, panic

clutching her chest. "We don't really want to fight, we just want to leave, but I can and will fight if I have to!"

Rhiannon shouted, "She has the queen's protection! Back away!"

"She has to help my mother!" Lady Morag's grasping hands wrenched at Darla's shirt.

A flash hurt Darla's eyes with a stabbing pain. Grabbing Rhiannon, Darla hunkered down, shielding her friend's head.

"Enough!" a large voice roared.

Blinking, Darla looked up at Rory, standing above them

He crouched, arms wide and claws out. His wet hair was plastered to his head with a swirl of wiry wet curls emblazoned on his chest, and a thick towel wrapped around his slim waist. Each cut of muscle was prominent as he held himself on the alert, ready to fight, and water droplets traced between the surge and swell of his back and shoulder muscles as he breathed. Darla's throat squeezed as if she had swallowed an urchin.

He slowly cracked his knuckles. "The charm on my guest's outfit was activated. What is happening here?"

The two women and the man backed away. "Nothing. Everything is fine," one said in a high voice.

Lady Morag's arms trembled against the stone flagons.

Rory leaned down, his torso overshadowing her. "Well? Lady Morag?"

She sat up, curls tumbling loose over her shoulders, her lips trembling. "She could help my mother."

Rory stilled. Why? Was he realizing she was a selkie as well?

Footsteps pounded down the street and Darla looked up to see Kater rounding the corner, taking in the scene. He looked to Darla and Rhiannon first, as if to make sure they were alright, then turned a wide smile at the fae backing away from them.

Rhiannon wriggled and Darla released her, so the woman could stand up. "I'm so sorry, Kater," Rhiannon whispered.

"What were you doing here, outside the market?" The tall man's gaze swept across the group again. His voice was even, not accusing, but Rhiannon clearly felt the rebuke, shrinking away.

Rory came to stand next to Kater, hands flexing with each deep exhalation as his chest rose and fell. Had he run here?

Kater bowed to Rory. "I rather think they won't be any trouble, Prince Rory."

Turning on his heel, Rory extended his hand to her. Darla took it, warmth surrounding her fingers at last, and he pulled her upright. "Are you alright?" he asked, voice low. His shoulders blocked the view behind him, creating an oasis of calm with his body. His half-naked body, wet from the baths with heat washing off him in waves, and all Darla wanted was to smooth along his side for comfort and shelter in his arms.

"I'm... fine." She wrenched her gaze off him and around his shoulder. The other fae had all calmed down now, but Lady Morag's eyes glittered with hope and want. Need, a grasping desire that Darla had seen in desperate selkies before: a look that meant that they would do anything to feed their children, to have their mate healed, to help their matriarch. The lady had a problem she intended to solve, and she seemed to think Darla could solve it.

"Come on. Let's get out of here." Rory's voice was low and thick with anger. Her cheek was pressed to his shoulder, her arms about his chest, and he was standing in very little clothes. She held him out at arm's length. "I thought Cat Sidhe insisted on clothing?"

His face finally cracked into a smile. A small one, yes, his jaw too tight to allow a full one to grace his face, but it sent a coil of warmth to her core all the same. "Yes, they do, but I was in the shower when the charms I laid on my jacket went off. Seems there was one to Kater as well."

Rhiannon had not been joking about the clothes having magic laced in them. Darla picked at her top. "Handy."

"Very. You can have me at a wave of your hand," he said, but there was a seriousness in his voice that spoke to Darla's core.

Rhiannon and Rory led Darla back to the castle, with Kater walking three steps behind them. Rory seemed to be nodding cordially to everyone they saw, but the mood ahead of them shifted; rather than keen interest in another potential customer, the merchants shrank back as if wary of being noticed, recoiling into their stalls as a sea snail did into their shell.

Rhiannon too was different, no longer hugging and hanging onto Darla's arm but keeping a handspan away from her. Darla wanted Rory to touch her again, but sometimes people needed space.

As they passed by the chocolate fountain shop, he cleared his throat. "Are you really alright?"

Darla considered the question properly, as he seemed to want her to. "I'm physically fine, a little shaken. My heart is beating kind of fast."

Rory nodded. "Adrenaline. Or being so close to me in this state." He spread his arms wide, glancing down at his naked torso. "Go on, you can look. Turnabout is fair play, after all."

Taking the invitation, Darla studied his body. The skin of his stomach was moulded with muscle, and his chest broadened to meet his wide shoulders. His pulse jumped in his throat, and his lips parted into a genuine smile. The princes and princesses in stories were pampered, placed carefully in pretty robes and palaces. Yet here was Rory, muscular form striding half-naked and barefoot through the marketplace even though fae preferred coverings. Maybe this was what being a prince meant here, doing whatever he wanted, whenever he wanted, but the fact he was hardened by work confused her. What did he do to look like he hunted all day every day?

Rhiannon nosed closer. "I'm surprised he hasn't asked you to feel his muscles yet."

Darla's face heated. "What a fascinating thing. But..." She bit her lip. His arms had folded so easily around her, cradling her like an otter wrapped in seaweed, protected from the waves. The lack now made the winds surrounding her colder. "I do have questions about what happened, though."

"Yes." Rory balled his hands into fists. "I expect you do."

Darla made sure to look into his eyes, holding his attention. "Did you know what I am?"

Rory's gaze flickered between her eyes, but he held her stare. "Orla knew and told me. I did not realise when we met." He looked away at last.

The truth he spoke vibrated pleasantly against Darla's cheeks. "Alright. I... I am not supposed to tell anyone what I am." Darla twisted her fingers in her hand. "I came up against the advice of my matriarchs." They had insisted on staying with the colony, but seeing the faces of the desperate Cat Sidhe surrounding them solidified that it was for her own protection.

"Matriarchs? So, there are more of you?" Rhiannon's eyes widened.

Darla's gut lurched in warning. Rhiannon had been nothing but friendly, but something about the hunger in the eyes of the fae they had just left made her vulnerable and wary. Really, how well did she know this place, its customs and norms, and especially its people?

"I'd love to meet more of you! You're so cute." Rhiannon's cheeks reddened to a rosy hue.

Darla looked back at Rory's hand, then hesitantly touched it. His large pale fingers wrapped around her darker hand. *You are safe, I have you,* she could imagine those big fingers saying to her trembling ones, and hers stilled.

She squeezed his hand in her own. "Who were those Cat Sidhe?"

Rory's pace quickened as if trying to put distance between them and Rhiannon. "Just some lesser nobles. The queen wants you to meet some worthies, but I wouldn't have put Lady Morag at the top of the list."

"Why does she want me to meet people?"

His gaze cut away. "You're an honoured guest."

The skin on Darla's cheeks tingled with a colder tremor than before. Some truth, and then something hidden behind the statement.

"And?" Darla pushed her nails into her palms. If Rory lied to her or refused to tell her, then who could she trust?

Rory let out a loud breath. A lock of his drying hair flopped onto his forehead, making him look playful, even though his expression was serious. "You recall I said that magic was leaving and the Worldheart was dying?"

Darla nodded. "Because it isn't being fed."

"Yes. It means our people are dying. They are becoming weak without magic, more likely to get ill." He met her eyes. "You, however, are one composed of something like the energy we find in souls, fresh and pure." His eyes met hers and his mouth worked. "Unmarked and unsullied by civilisation, I mean," he stammered.

Seeing him struggle to find the words gave Darla a light feeling in her chest. "What does that correlate with?"

His expression was grave. "You are radiant. You exude energy." His throat bobbed. "You're like... freshwater, when all we have had is brackish pond scum for centuries."

"I exude energy?" Darla studied her hands. "How?"

"I don't know."

Darla could hardly stop the eager jump of her thoughts. "Is there someone who does know?"

Rory's jaw worked. There were big shadows under his eyes. If she smoothed her fingers over them, would they fade away?

"Orla probably knows," Rory said quietly. He was close enough that the words brushed over Darla's cheeks. It would be simple to press her lips to his, if she wanted…

Until he opened his mouth and ruined it. "I'm in charge tomorrow," he admonished Rhiannon sharply.

"Yes, Prince Rory," she said in a small voice, and Darla's stomach turned. She hated bullies!

Rory shook his hand at Darla. "No more crowds. Got it?"

Darla bared her teeth briefly as Rory turned away and stalked off.

CHAPTER 12

Rory

Rory paced, still pissed a crowd had been bold enough to try to pull Darla away for themselves. How dare someone try to steal her! The charm on the jacket alerted him in time, but Kater appearing as well was very valuable information. It meant Orla was being very, very careful with their guest. *My guest, not Orla's. She is my responsibility.* The image of Darla crouched on the ground protecting Rhiannon sent a spike of fear deep into Rory's chest.

"Hey, brother." Kade leaned out from the doorway to the kitchens, munching on a sandwich. They did not look much alike, sandy haired to Rory and Orla's rich red, and while his twin used his wits and wiles to charm just as much as Rory, he somehow seemed more earnest about it. He was genuine in his compliments in a way Rory just didn't feel anymore; he and his brother could do the same favour for someone, but Rory always lodged it to collect later on down the line whereas Kade seemed genuinely happy to help.

Swallowing his mouthful, Kade brushed crumbs off his immaculate shirt. "You okay? You look..."

Rory rolled his eyes. "No need to search for some poetic and polite way to say I look like shit."

"I wasn't going to say that! I heard you brought someone back from the human realm! Some kind of new fae?"

"Maybe." Rory frowned and looked over Kade's shoulder; Kade turned and Rory snagged his snack. "Oldest trick in the book," he admonished with a tut before taking a bite.

Kade scowled. "Unlike you, I don't expect family to run their tricks just for the hell of it. Are you in need of practice or something? Why don't you stab me in vulnerable areas while you're at it?"

The bread was chewy, Rory's jaw working overtime, and the cheese old and hard. Was this really the best the kitchens could do? No: Kade probably took the older stock so he wouldn't be a bother, saving the good things for someone who needed it. Sometimes Kade's kind heart caused Rory to bleed inside.

Handing the sandwich back, Rory finished his pilfered bite. "I regret it. That tasted half a week old."

Kade ruffled his hair. Blond to Rory's red, the twins did not look much alike. "That's what you get for stealing." Sliding an arm around his shoulders, Kade steered him toward the back door. "So," he continued, voice low, "tell me about this new fae. Orla said she was a selkie."

Rory glared at the bright light stabbing his eyes as they spilled out into the walled garden. "I'm not sure she is, I'm pretty sure I've smelled something like her before."

Kade gave him a sharp look, this time genuinely insulted. "Don't give me that."

"What?" Rory tried to widen his eyes, feigning innocence.

Kade's arm dropped from his back. "Rory, it's *me*. I can tell when you're lying to me, you prick, and we're alone." He looked away quickly but not before Rory caught the hurt there.

Argh. Bloody bleeding heart. "Fine, alright, but keep your voice down. Yes, she's a selkie, and a magnet for trouble. She's like catnip to Cat Sidhe, she feels like a bundle of souls all just ready to be swiped up and carted away." He could even feel it now, a steady glow against his soul sense. "Lady Morag was this close to snatching her off the street yesterday."

"I can't feel anything from here, so don't fret." Kade took another bite, giving Rory a considering look. Unfortunately, Kade's soul sense was less developed than Rory's, so the reassurance didn't land. "Is that why you look like you haven't slept all night?"

"Sleep is for the weak." Rory shoved his hands deeper into his pockets, fingers turning over the condensed magic within. He hadn't had to use a single one near Darla. "She... she has this kind of energy. Exudes it. Makes you feel and act like you collected a million souls and you're rolling in them."

"Mm." Kade's eyebrow twitched. "What else?"

Rory clicked the beads together in his pocket. "She's just so full of life, she's bouncing with it, dripping with it. You know how mortals are, that *go faster get everything* energy because they know they're on a timer, and it's kind of like that, except different. She sees everything anew, Kier, and it's all fresh and wonderful, but she's not exactly naïve either. She's... curious about everything, wants to know how it works, how it came to be, what it does, it's purpose. Everything."

Kade linked arms with him, tugging towards the glasshouse. "Sounds lovely. Tell me more."

"She asks good questions but also odd ones, and it makes me stop and question it too." Rory's gaze slid over the meagre plants the Cat Sidhe had managed to encourage out here. "And she's unfazed by anything, yet free to display whatever emotions she's feeling. Imagine entering a completely new world and greeting it with eager abandon, like some kind of happy explorer."

"She sounds delightful. I can't wait to meet her."

Rory's steps slowed. "Perhaps we can act as a tour guide somewhere."

"And be the third wheel? No thanks." Kade winked at Rory. "I'd hate to come between you as you're making moon eyes at her."

Shoving his shoulder, Rory scowled at his twin. "There's nothing to come between! Jeez, I only met her yesterday."

Kade counted on his fingers. "And pulled her through saving her from human law enforcement, and then stopped the Cat Sidhe from getting over zealous, again rescuing her–"

"Being a good host," Rory insisted.

"And just now waxed lyrical with the most poetic words and wistful face I've ever seen on you."

Rory groaned. "Don't say it."

"Love! My little brother has fallen in love at last!" He wrapped his arms around Rory's neck, sandwich and all.

"Gerroff," Rory grumbled. He didn't want to shove him, but Kade clung too hard. "I doubt it."

"I don't!" Kade laughed, his joy echoing back from the decaying walls of the stronghold.

Seeing his delight, Rory couldn't help but crack a smile. Just a small one. "Don't get your knickers in a twist."

"Love is the most beautiful thing in the world, and absolutely something to get your knickers in a twist over." Kade put his hands on his hips. "Just don't screw up."

"I can't help but screw up anyone near me," Rory muttered, scanning the walls.

Kade cocked his head. "That's not true, Riri."

That tugged like a true name for Rory, the moniker Kade had first called him when they were learning to speak. "No baby names," he warned. "You're getting entirely too excited. She's just visiting, I'm trying to be a good host and make sure our guest leaves with all limbs attached."

Kade sighed. "You're missing out, Rory. One day I hope

you'll see that love isn't a burden or a weakness. It's literally the purpose of my life, the core of my being." He gazed out over the tumbledown walls at the light warming the sky.

Rory held back from teasing his brother. *If that were true, all our problems would be solved already.* Still, seeing his brother passionate about something, anything or anyone, gave Rory a tiny bit of relief from the unrelenting burden pressing on them all.

However, reality would not be denied. "So bringing the conversation back to something *useful*, I have to find something to do with our guest that scratches her itch for exploration and yet doesn't expose her to more grabby-handed fae."

Kade seemed to be lost in thought, staring beyond the Cat Sidhe walls. Rory nudged him. "Kier? Are you composing a sonnet or something?"

He rubbed the abused spot absently. "No, not exactly. Thinking." He shook himself. "You'll figure it out, Rory, I've got somewhere I need to be. Duty calls!"

"What duty?"

"Not sure yet, just where my heart leads me." Kade used misdirection and vague statements, and this felt like half a lie to Rory. Maybe a white lie, so Rory wouldn't worry.

"Right." Rory pulled the marbles out of his pocket, thrusting them at his brother. "Take these, I don't need them right now."

Kade's eyes widened, the glow of the beads reflecting back. "This is a lot of magic, Riri!"

"Yep, only the finest for Orla's best soul seeker." He made it sound like an honour he was proud of rather than a vocation chipping away at his charred heart. If Kade could tell a white lie so Rory wouldn't worry, he could do the same to him.

"I can charge my garnet with this." Kade pulled out a dark purple stone, the facets angled to give the impression of a sly face. The stone absorbed the concentrated magic, glowing with dark purpose. "My thanks, Rory."

"Sure." Hopefully that garnet would disguise him for whatever mission he undertook next, "Happy hunting."

"You too." Kade tossed the garnet in the air and caught it, grinning ear to ear. "Can't wait to hear more about her."

"Who?" Rory said, to see his brother's reaction.

With a roll of his eyes, Kade leapt up the side of the wall and away. Kade was the better climber, not that Rory would ever admit it to him, and certainly the only one able to scale the gardens. How did he find even the smallest of leverage so quickly?

It did give Rory an idea, though. He rubbed his hands. "Alright, Darla. You've met your match. One safe expedition, coming up."

CHAPTER 13
Darla

Darla had spent the night reading the books Rhiannon brought for her. There wasn't time for much sleep, there was too much to explore, too much of the realm to experience. Rather than the grating hiss of the waves, there were people chattering, footsteps clattering, laughter and music. Sure, selkies had some of those too, but secretive and secluded. Here, everyone seemed free to do as they wished all the time.

Stretching, Darla got up and peered out of the window at the sky turning pink to welcome the sun. No horses today but a barrel being rolled out of the piecemeal walls of the castle, two Cat Sidhe youths whooping as it gained speed. Like coral, this place had an irregular shape, but it thrived, blooming with life.

Jumping in and out of the tub to refresh herself, Darla looked critically over at the wardrobe. More of those smaller shirts presented themselves: one said, "Touch me and die," in blood red, the other, "Look but don't linger," in a bright sunny yellow. Darla's stomach flipped. Rory was only protecting her, yes? It wasn't anything more than that. Right?

She pulled on the *Look but don't linger* one. It fitted her sentiment here anyway: to see as much as she could, not staying too long in case she missed something else happening in another part of this fascinating world. Pulling her jeans up, she opened the door. "Hey," a voice said, and Darla nearly leaped backward.

Rory raised his hands where he lounged against the opposite wall. "It's only me, and I didn't even try to jump out at you."

"I wasn't expecting you to be right there, right that heartbeat." Her own heart flapped like a landed fish. "Were you... there all night?"

Rory chuckled, the sound dark and low. "That would be impractical. No, I wasn't here all night. Who would protect entry through the windows?"

Truth tingled against Darla's cheeks, discomfort bubbling up her chest. Of course a prince wouldn't guard outside her door all night! He had far more important things to do.

She picked at her shirt. "Was this you?"

He took the invitation to look at her chest. "Mm, nice. What was your question, or did you just want to show off your form again?"

She gently shoved his shoulder. "Never mind, you're in some sort of contrary mood."

He laughed. "Guilty as charged, on both counts. Kater was trying to make you some unenchanted clothes, so I took over to provide style advice." Rory turned in place, the spin sending his coat to flare, like some kind of fish fin. "Now then, I have an action packed day planned, so pack your sightseeing eyes."

A thrill raced across Darla's nerves. "You? You're taking me somewhere?"

"No one else could keep up with you, I assure you." He led the way down the stairs, past all the plant life trying to squirm its way in.

"Where to? Where is it? How far? What will we see on the

way?" Darla caught up to him, holding onto his sleeve to make sure they stayed together.

He let out a burst of laughter. "All your questions and more shall be answered, but in reverse." He gestured up at the great hall of the castle, the sky blue with white wisps racing across it. "We will see this piece of history, the echoes of former glory still just about audible if you listen hard enough." He tapped a stone archway, leading her past Queen Orla's study, and pointed down the hallway. "The throne room, possibly the most expensive one in the whole fae realm if you include lives in that analysis."

Darla slowed, the delighted smile on her face falling. "Pardon?"

Rory hitched his cheery smile higher. "Never mind! On your right you will see the door which we do not open." He leaned down to whisper in Darla's ear. "Not because there's anything vicious or terrifying behind it, but because the lintel sunk and it is literally stuck closed."

Darla nodded, unsure what expression to wear on her face, and settling for guarded bemusement.

"And here..." Rory flourished his hands in rapid waving movements. Was he trying to fly? Darla copied him in an attempt to understand, and the genuine amusement in his face made her heart pound a little harder.

He let his hands fall. "Alright, I'll stop teasing you. Ready for the surprise?"

Darla nodded eagerly.

"Good, but it has to be a surprise. Turn around, I'll put my hands over your eyes and guide you toward it. Ready?"

"Yes." Darla turned without hesitation, trembling with excitement.

He stepped up behind her slowly. Warmth flooded her chest, and he wasn't even touching her yet! His voice murmured, "So trusting, just like that?"

"Mm, yes?" She looked over her shoulder at him. "Shouldn't I be?"

He stared at her, arms raised ready to cup his hands over her face. His expression was guarded surprise, like a bull seal finally allowed into the harem.

He admitted, "I'm not used to it, is all." He opened his mouth to say more, then twirled his finger, indicating she should turn back around.

Darla did so, standing straight as his big palms lowered over her eyes. He smelled good, warm and earthy. She expected his scent to be similar to the castle, but they smelled very different, almost as if he spent little time in his home.

His arms put a little pressure on her shoulders. "Onward!" Darla walked and he was right behind her, chest brushing her back, but he was careful never to step on her heels. "Whoa, there," he murmured in her ear. "Make sure you raise your feet for the next step. I suppose I haven't done anything–yet–to make you regret your choice to trust me on Earth, so I'd better make sure you don't stub your toe."

"Thank you." She felt her way forward. "Plus they are still only a few days old, seems a shame to bruise them so early on."

"Absolutely. Can't invalidate the warranty in the first week."

"Do what to who?"

"Nevermind." Rory chuckled. "A complicated human expression."

"Ah, I see." She slowed as Rory's arms steered her portside. "So, am I allowed to guess where we are going?"

"Certainly. Mind the edge here, let me just..." Rory slid himself next to her and guided her past. Her skin brushed against his, an electric shiver in the wake of his warmth against her cold arm. "There. So, let's try for three guesses."

"Why only three?"

He hesitated for a moment. "Call it a cultural artefact."

"Does that mean you don't know?"

"Me? A being of incredible age and experience, not knowing something like this? Of course I know."

The lie would have made Darla's whiskers wilt, but in this form it tickled her cheeks. He only wanted to impress her, though, not deceive her to hurt, so Darla let it slide. "You don't know," she said smugly. "You can admit it."

"Admit a failing to a beauty? Never!"

Now Darla giggled, holding on to Rory's hands so they wouldn't accidentally slip off her eyes and ruin the surprise. "Alright, three guesses. A portal to somewhere else?"

"No. Cat Sidhe can only open portals randomly. We were lucky as fuck to open one right into a patch I happened to recognise, so I could tear us another one out." Gentle pressure steered her to port again. "Took all my magic, though. Good job I have incredible endurance."

His voice was low enough to send tingles down Darla's spine, as well as the tickle of a slight lie. "You seemed to get a lot of something when I touched you."

"Mm, that I did. You can touch me anytime and see if it has the same effect. For science!"

Darla couldn't cover her smiling mouth, still holding onto his warm hands over her eyes, but he hadn't seemed to take seeing her teeth before as a threat. Her nose caught some kind of food, her stomach snarling, but Rory guided her away and then... back again?

He didn't say anything further for a moment, steps speeding up. Their pathway echoed, so they were still inside the castle somewhere. "You have two more guesses."

"What happens if I guess wrong?"

"Is that one of the guesses? No, that's silly, Rory," he admonished himself. "How about, I get to ask you questions?"

"That seems fair," she replied. "Even if I lose, I'm happy to answer questions." Her cheeks heated. "Well, not questions about where I came from. That's not happening."

"Very well, that's off the table. You know I'm going to ask you how attractive I am, right?"

This time she couldn't help but spin in place to confront him. The light, although dim, was bright after she had spent so long with her eyes closed, so she had to squint at Rory's outline. She put her hands on her hips to match his pose. "You meet a new fae and all you want to ask is how attractive they find you?"

His eyes flickered with mirth and something else, a self-deprecating twinkle. "Yep. I'm horrendously shallow, as well as having incredible endurance."

Darla stared up at him. His eyes shifted in color from the rich brown of kelp to the warning tone of an anemone. He believed what he was saying, but it still rang a little hollow. "That's not all you are."

He blinked, the only show of his surprise. "And how do you know?"

"I just know." She pointed behind her shoulder. "Same as I know we are heading around in circles, but our destination is probably where I can smell the food coming from." Before Rory could catch her, she raced toward the enticing scent. It led her outside, the light bright and making her slow to shield her sensitive eyes. Once she'd blinked back her stinging tears, she gasped.

This was some kind of enclosed area, the walls more solid. A gentle hill rolled down to a structure all in glass, and Darla's senses filled with *life*. Vibrant, living, vital and here! Plants curled up and down the walls, flowers nodding in the breeze, all shapes, sizes, colors and, oh, the fragrances! Sweet and enticing, lush and heady. Entranced, she stepped forward toward the delicious smells. "What is all of this?"

Rory thumped down onto a checked blanket, laid out in the sun. He pointed as he explained, "Bread rolls, fresh out of the oven. Pork slices here, what's left of the beef joint over there."

"Bread!" Darla had only read about it. "How do you eat it?"

Rory picked out one of the steaming stone like objects, which actually looked to be light-weight, and tossed it into the air. When it landed he tore it in two and then presented it to Darla.

"Huh." Darla picked her own. It was soft and pliant. She threw it up, but it arched away from them and bounced down the hill. She quickly scrambled after it, Rory bursting into a low chuckle.

Grabbing it with both hands, she trotted back. "That's not as easy as it looked."

"Indeed." He cut a chunk off a pale yellow block and held it up for her. "Cheese."

She sniffed it, then took it in her mouth. A creamy sharp tang exploded on her tongue. "Oh my."

Rory cleared his throat. "Oh my indeed."

She sat next to him. "How do you make that?"

"We don't, we steal it." Rory laid back, closing his eyes. "We take what we can get, and then go for that bit extra."

Darla chewed slowly, the cheese turning to paste. "What do you mean?"

He cracked an eye open. "We have to. We don't have a court to call our own, no claim to a gemstone mine and therefore, no wealth."

"No... wealth?" Darla looked around at the beautiful boun-tiful garden, the rich food laid in front of her.

Rory snorted. "You've seen the Cat Sidhe home, our little castle no one else wanted. Hell, there's a tree growing out of our main street." His eyelids clenched along with his fists, as if he was seeing something behind his eyes that offended him. "No court means no power, and we can be evicted from this place once the owner decides they want it back."

Darla swallowed the cheese. "Are you nomadic?"

His eyelid slowly opened, like a mussel testing the waters

before relaxing it's shell. "Maybe, but every bugger else has a court and some kind of claim to a gemstone mine."

Like the stone he had used to heal her. "If you don't have a resource in your territory, you can't trade, but you also don't get attacked for it," she mused.

"No one threatens a court that has an infinite supply of fire rubies or kyanite to attack your mind, or even emeralds to over-stimulate healing and give you an autoimmune disease. Us?" He snorted. "We have the few gems we've *acquired,* and then try to recharge them using magic."

Darla took a slice of meat. It was cold and these new teeth were ill-suited to tearing it. Rory watched her attempts to rip the food, face evaluating. "Once you're done with this meager breakfast, we can explore the greenhouse." He pointed to the structure glittering at the foot of the hill.

"Meager?" It didn't look small at all, bread, cheeses and meats sufficient for the pair of them.

"Mm," he snorted with some of that cutting self-deprecation. "It's no feast, but we take what we can get, eh? That's practically the Cat Sidhe creed."

A prickle laced Darla's stomach, and she put the bread down. "I don't want to take too much if this is all you have. Thank you for sharing it with me."

In an instant, he sat up, intent. "Don't worry about it, forget I said anything. This is all for you, I just..." He looked away, down at the glittering glasshouse. "I just wish it was more."

More, when this feast was one of Darla's limited meals on the surface, her first taste of fabled cheese! She took another bite, thinking. "Perspective really is everything. This is a wonderful feast of firsts for me," she explained.

"Yes, I suppose. I have no desire to disappoint."

She swallowed hard, the lump in her throat sliding down slowly as her cheeks heated. He was nice to look at in a humanoid form, and her new body definitely agreed with that statement. Plus his kindness now, and the fact he was upset he couldn't do more.

Focus, Darla. Look but don't linger.

But while she could, she would enjoy the looking.

Darla bounced up, extending her hands out for him. "Glasshouse, please!"

He folded his fingers around her hands, only pulling slightly as he got to his feet. "As the lady commands, so it shall be." He held out his arm and Darla copied him, bumping forearms with him, but he took her hand and swooped it under his arm and up over to rest on his forearm like a seal basking on a rock. This close, her hip slid alongside Rory's, and the frisson soaring through her was undeniable. Well, she could play for a short time, couldn't she?

The glasshouse rose low and long across the bottom of the hill, glittering in the suntrap between the walls and the castle like a gem. Inside sat rows of orderly plants in small tubs. Rory slid the door open to a rush of heat that washed over Darla's skin like a current, and they stepped into a cacophony of scents, too thick to catalogue and hanging in the heat. Moisture clouded the air, coating her hair instantly as she breathed in the heat, almost thick enough to chew. She pulled at her vest as sweat sprung up on her chest and arms, and Rory let out a loud breath. "That's one heck of a temperature difference."

"What is this place?" Darla trailed her hand along the wicker tables. The pots nearby were decorated with smudges of dirt, with heady loam inside their bowls, while the ones further along had thin green stems stretching for the ceiling. Darla inhaled deeply, mouth open to taste the air. The steam was rich with thick, earthy scents and sweeter scents from the greenery further inside the glasshouse.

"It's a nursery for plants." Rory pointed her toward a sprig barely pushing up above the soil. "A lot seems to be fading from the fae world. My brother Kade thinks it might be linked to plant life, either as an effect or the cause." He shook his head. Sunlight drenched his hair, glinting on shades of rust red and gold as iridescent as any shell.

"And you don't think so?"

"Nope." The 'p' rang hard between them. Was that bitterness or despair Darla could hear in his voice? "I leave grubbing in the dirt to Kade, but at least he has–" He broke off, staring at the plant.

Darla's palms tingled as the plant sprung up underneath her hands. A bright green glow pulsed steadily behind the tables. Ducking, Darla found a bank of green glittering stones in leaf shapes.

"The emeralds," Rory said, now breathless with wonder. That tone rang much better in Darla's ears. "They are... What's happening?"

"They don't often do that?" The green brightened, like seeing the sunrise under the waves.

"Never." Rory sucked in a breath as the plants thrust upward, stems thickening, leaves unfurling, buds sprouting and opening. Surrounded by scents and color, Darla laughed, dragging Rory further into the glasshouse. Toward the back were the bigger plants, saplings surging into thick trunks, flower heads ripening into fruit, and all around that green glow getting deeper.

And deeper.

A tree thrust out of a crack in the ground, separating her from Rory, and plants writhed as they grew faster and faster, spilling out onto the floor and over her feet. Ceramic cracked with the snap of a rock slide, pinging shards into Darla's stomach. "Ow!"

"Darla!" Rory shouted, then swore. "The emeralds are overcharging, everything is growing too fast!"

"Why are they–" A vine boiled over the plants around it,

tendrils latching onto her arm. It tightened, wrapping around as if she were a fish caught in tentacles. "Um. Help?"

"Some of these are poisonous, don't let them touch you."

"Too late!" Darla yanked backward from the bank of plants. More unfurled and spread, over her head, rubbing leathery leaves over her cheeks and neck. Flowers unraveled right in her face, blinding her with pollen, and Darla choked.

A hard clamp around her arm made her scream and flail, but the pull dragged her out of her cave of plants. She looked up at Rory's strained face. He stood on top of the squirming tree, lifting her out. He whipped around, then pointed at the tree pushing against the glass roof. "There! Just be ready to cover your face." Taking her hand, he ran up the side of the twisting tree, ducking underneath the hot glass. Darla followed and he held her upright on the rolling trunk.

The glass strained, a crack wending down a pane as the tree pushed against it, as inexorable as the incoming tide. He pulled her head against his chest and lashed out upwards against the glass. The crash as it smashed was shortly followed by a shower of shards, and Darla burrowed closer to Rory's racing heartbeat.

He stood but she was anchored down and slipped from his arms. Vines curled around her legs, binding them together as if she were back to being a seal, pressing tightly as they roamed up her torso. All she could do was lift her arms. "Go."

"Bugger that." Long claws shot out from his fingertips as he slashed at the grasping plants winding around her waist, the edges fearsome as jagged rocks. He didn't nick her at all, and his claws receded as he wrapped his hands around her upper arms. "Kick, Darla!"

As he heaved upward she bucked as if she were flapping her tail to the surface. Her legs slid free and Rory hauled her into his arms. He used his fist to dislodge the remaining pieces of glass hampering their escape, each falling to smash against the heaving tree below. As they rose, Rory kept her locked against his hard body, and then he leapt up and out of the greenhouse.

He stood on the roof, casting about for the best way down. Branches smashed through more panels one after the other below them. "We have to get you away from the emeralds, so you'll stop overfilling them."

"I didn't mean to."

"I know, but right now, we need to get down." He sucked in a breath. "This is a very strange question for me to ask, but just in case: can you climb?"

"I don't think so. Can you?"

His jaw ticked. "Yes. Follow me." Taking her hand he ran, Darla swept up behind him. He dodged before more branches shot out of his path, cutting to the side and keeping his body between her and the enthusiastic plants. Underneath their steps the plants were so thick the glass seemed green, that eerie glow glimmering underneath the roiling plant life.

He pulled up where the roof of the greenhouse met the walls surrounding the castle, crumbling stonework a barrier between the gardens and the town. Darla bent down to look over the side, blocks wobbling underneath her hands. Rory yanked her back.

She gulped. "Is this safe?"

"Safer," he allowed, flexing his hands and taking a deep breath. His eyes locked on the drop right at their feet as he lowered to his haunches. "Get on my back and hold on."

Wrapping her arms around his shoulders, Darla leaned flush against him. His back muscles slid like smooth waves underneath her hips, stomach and breasts.

He turned, back to the wall. The roof they'd traversed was buckling, inexorably pressed upwards in a huge swell. "Ready?" He twisted his neck to meet her eyes. "I won't let you get hurt."

Her cheeks tingled with truth. He would never. "Alright, I'm ready."

Rory backed up a pace, took a deep breath, and hopped. Darla's arms clamped in a stranglehold as they dropped over the wall, grey filling her vision accompanied by a loud screech.

They slowed and came to a halt, Rory gasping. His claws dug into the joins between the stones, shoulders quivering with the effort of holding them suspended above the drop. Slowly he retracted one hand—he had to be incredibly strong to hold them with only one!—and placed it lower down before extracting the other one. Hand over hand he got them lower and lower, legs braced against the wall, Darla dangling off his back. Heat pushed against her from his body, his muscles hard sliding rocks under her cheeks and chest as he worked, and the heat somehow made its way between her legs, pulsing in time with her heart. He was sweating and straining to keep them safe, to take her to safely. She nuzzled his neck, taking in the salty scent of his exertion, and the pants he was making changes in timbre.

"Do that again, it's distracting," he panted.

"Is distracting you a good idea?" She eyed the drop below them, still a good distance between them and the marketplace. She could make out the stallholders faces, but not their expressions, turned up pointing at them descending the walls of the castle.

His breath hitched. "I, uh, I'll tell you something, but you... you must keep it secret."

"Alright."

"I..." He swallowed hard, his panting ragged. "I'm afraid of heights."

A smile stole across Darla's face, the heat in her body from his deepening. He was afraid and doing it anyway, to save them. Her.

She brought her lips to his ear. "Mm. You don't look afraid."

His motions became smoother, gaining a rhythm of feel for a purchase, slide down, unhook his claws above them, feel below. "Well, I have to be fearless in front of a beautiful fae."

Darla barked with laughter even as the heat between her legs became an insistent throb. "So are you saying I'm a nice distraction?"

"Yes." His voice was firm despite his breathlessness. "So keep distracting me."

Darla couldn't really do anything except cling to him, but she wrapped her legs around his waist. He sucked in a breath and she halted, but he said in a strained tone, "Carry on."

"Alright, well..." Darla looked around for inspiration of what to talk about. "The sun is heading toward midday. This will be my second day on the surface and in the fae realm, and so far it's been fascinating." Her hips rode over Rory's rippling back, and she snuggled closer. "I love learning about magic and all the history here. I'd need several lifetimes, let alone days, to explore everything there is to see here."

Rory grunted. "It's surprisingly samey after a while."

"No, there'll be something unique about everything. There is no plant, place or person ever exactly the same as anywhere else."

He chuckled. "Well, I certainly hope this experience is unique."

Darla bit her lip. "It really is."

"I aim to please." He chanced a look down. "Oh, thank Arawn of the Otherworld, we're nearly there."

Darla twisted to see, craning her neck over her shoulder. Below the stallholders had gathered into quite the little group, gawking upwards like seagulls, and now she could see their disbelief and consternation.

"They don't look very happy."

"They'll put it down to another one of my antics." Rory eased them down further, grunting as his boot slipped on the sheer side of a stone. His throat bobbed and Darla was acutely aware of how close they were, how her cheek rubbed his neck as he moved, how the hairs on his chin looked short and sharp but the hairs on his chest had looked rough and coarse. What would each feel like along her sensitive skin?

His claws retracted, silver scars crisscrossing his knuckles. What did those rivulets feel like? Would they be silky smooth like the silver Worldheart necklace she had been given? What would those hands, so adept, so strong, feel like on running the length of her body?

"Here you are, lass." Other hands reached up to support her, and she found herself lifted from Rory's back and set on the ground.

Rory let go and landed, shaking out his arms and grimacing, and turned around immediately to face the merchants milling around her. "Back away."

"Prince Rory, what are you up to now?" a woman said with a laugh, but her amusement froze on her face. She sniffed the air. "What is that? Where is it coming from?"

Even though his body had to be aching with exhaustion, Rory put himself between her and the stallholders. "There is nothing to see here. Nothing at all!"

"Oh, Rory, what a way to talk of our guest." Queen Orla, closely followed by Kater, came into the knot of Cat Sidhe from the castle. Her eyes sparkled as she talked to her subjects in a soothing voice, "There will be an event tonight where you can ask questions of us, and of course we have to welcome our visitor." Orla winked at Darla. "No one does parties like Cat Sidhe."

Darla ducked her head. "You don't have to, but thank you."

"Oh, but I do," Orla purred.

"Is that wise?" Rory hissed bluntly at his sister.

Orla's teeth flashed in her mouth, gaze pointedly going over the group surrounding them. They looked excited, energised, all of them looking at her. The plants in the greenhouse has seemed to be reaching for her too, like she was a source of sunlight. She wanted to wrap her arms around Rory's strong shoulders again.

"Very," Orla said quietly.

CHAPTER 14

Rory

Rory paced outside Darla's room, fighting the urge to rip the door open. She'd been in there for hours now, doing Arawn only knew what with hair or outfits. Enough time for Rory to knock back a drink to get over the horrendous height he'd dangled not only his sorry ass over, but Darla's as well. Thinking of Darla holding on so tight, how she'd smoothed her cheek to his neck, how she'd trusted him to get them down safely, sent tingles down his spine.

He'd also had time to bathe and shave and dress in the red dinner jacket and slacks laid out for him, and Darla still wasn't done, and his ire still wasn't abated. Orla had interfered too much; Darla was his responsibility, and now he had to take her to a damned ball.

Throwing a big party was something Orla loved doing, but was this really the way to announce the most important discovery in centuries? Every Cat Sidhe would want to bask in some of Darla's energy, to feel her effects up close, to marvel at her. Was Orla trying to please her people, or show them what she had access to? Was this a way to cool off any protest about

Darla hidden away by letting people experience what her presence could do for them, or would it only bring desires to a boil?

Rory's own wants were running unchecked, rampant. Darla was the brightest thing in his life right now. Was he trying to protect her, or was he selfishly keeping her to himself?

The door cracked open, and Rory turned eagerly to see her at last.

Rhiannon walked out first, pretty as usual in a green silk dress that brought out the golden colour of her eyes. Rhiannon was nice enough for a fae, said to make human friends rather than bait them for sport, and she clearly cared for the people that Orla gave her to as a companion. Rory suspected she passed around castle gossip, but that was advantageous sometimes.

Rhiannon flounced right up to him. "You're going to explode."

Rory frowned. "Your pardon?"

"Explode. Poof." Rhiannon spread her fingers to demonstrate. "Look."

Darla stepped into the doorway.

Her hair was loose, a dark halo around her head. Her eyes were luminous, outlined with striking pinks and yellows. She wore a fantastic billowing skirt that draped to the floor and clung to her hips. Criss-crossing ribbons of crimson red and golden yellow made up the top of the dress and her midriff lay exposed.

Rory startled when Rhiannon tapped the bottom of his chin. "What?"

"Close your mouth. You're drooling like a dog," Rhiannon said with an evil smile.

Snapping his jaw shut, Rory took a step forward, the movements jerky. *Damn it, I'm centuries old, I cannot be nervous around a woman!* He knew a thousand millions ways to pleasure a partner, up, down, left, right and sideways, had plumbed every depth of carnal desire until left utterly drained and devoid of passion for... well. Too long.

Because every single one of those feelings welled up again, familiar as old friends long forgotten, as new and cutting as a sharp bright blade.

No. No! It hurts too much. Rory tried to tamp it down from long experience, but it was too tempting to lean toward into Darla, her cool touch as refreshing and enlivening as being drenched in a wild waterfall.

He held out his arm, and as she took it he refused to accept how her touch made his heart stutter and leap. She made everyone feel that way; it was just her way. How her bright eyes found his, and that crooked smile...

"Oh, that is bad," Rhiannon murmured behind him.

He resisted the urge to kick in her direction.

"Hello," Darla said.

"Hell—" Rory began, but she put her hand to his shoulder, stood on her tiptoes, and pressed her cheek against his.

Rory stood stock still, those feelings roaring inside him. He could smell her, hear her soft skin rasping against some scrap of stubble he hadn't managed to get while shaving, feel the cool calm of her touch, see right down that dress-wrap thing to the sweet, shadowed retreat between her breasts. *Grab her, kiss her, take her far from here!*

She dropped back onto her heels. "How are you? You're warm."

Only from his vast experience of enduring centuries of boredom could he pull a note of dull but steady calm into his voice. "Darla." Her name tasted good in his mouth. She would taste better.

A small line appeared between her eyebrows. "Yes?"

"We should... I should... that is..."

"Darla!" Orla's voice rang out down the corridor.

Rory's shoulder blades twitched, and he locked his jaw shut. *How did Orla know her name?*

He swivelled his glare to Rhiannon, but the small fae wasn't paying attention to him, curtseying at Orla.

Orla held Darla at arm's length. "My, you look beautiful, darling. Very Egyptian pharaoh meets twenties sparkle." Orla wore a yellow and red gown, the colors matching Darla. "And Rory, there you are. Put a smile on your face, why don't you? Well, let's get started, shall we?"

Orla escorted Darla, and Rory walked beside Rhiannon. The little fae chattered happily to Rory, no sense of guilt if she had told Orla Darla's true name, but he barely heard her, only enough to offer rote replies to her observations about the day's weather.

He kept an eye on Darla and Orla, how the two walked arm in arm, with Orla matching Darla's strides and keeping up with Darla's questions. As they filtered toward the main hall, the numbers of fae increased, and Rory kept watch against them too, nerves singing and claws ready to shoot out.

These were families, children hanging onto their parents' hands as the adults lined up to drop them at their own special party. Orla greeted the children all by name, gently brushing cheeks with the parents and ruffling the little one's hair.

Rory's tension relaxed around the children. They knew how to take life in their stride, curious and playful without that cruel edge born of boredom.

"Do you know everyone in the realm?" Darla was asking Orla, and Rory shook his maudlin thoughts away.

Orla smiled. "Near enough. How much do you understand of cats?"

Darla glanced up at him, and oh, hells, but his dead heart was coming back to life in the glory of her gaze. "Rory is the first I've met. They purr, don't they?"

"Oh, so you made my brother purr, eh?" Orla laughed.

Rory clenched his fists. Orla would use this somehow!

Orla continued, "It's a common misconception that we are solitary. Cats hunt in bonded pairs and form family groupings, raising children communally under an alliance of dominant females." Orla broke off to gently disengage a little girl's hands from her skirts. "In a way, they are all our children, and we are all their parents."

"That sounds the same as us!" Darla put a hand to her mouth.

Orla slipped her arm around Darla's shoulders. "Oh yes? I confess, I don't know how your kind is organised. That is interesting, but it means we are closer than I thought." Orla pressed her cheek to Darla's. "I can tell one thing is the same. We have a need to cuddle, to bond with colony mates and share a scent-identity, despite any impression Rory may have given you."

Darla's gaze darted toward him, and Rory shook a smile into place. "I can be cuddly when called for." But in truth his body was stiff, the same thoughts racing through his head. The children were being shooed away to their creche, where they would be treated to games and too many sweets. Their hearts would be achingly full, but Rory's hurt. They didn't know their world was dying and would look unrecognisable when they were older.

A frown creased Darla's forehead. Could she sense his agitation? It must be bleeding out to everyone within a two-mile radius. It didn't help that the adult fae had started swarming toward Orla to greet their queen and, even more eagerly, meet the guest of honour.

"Let us through." Orla spoke with a smile, but clear command underlined her words. The Cat Sidhe parted, and Rory saw even more hovering at the edges of the corridor, the nobles arm-in-arm with older fae. The vulnerable, the elderly, and infirm had expended a huge effort to come tonight. Rory seethed. There were too many people and even though he stole souls to feed into the Worldheart to sustain them all, and it was never enough. And now he had to give them Darla? A surge of strength pushed through his tiredness, and his hands balled into fists to hide his claws sliding out.

The throne room's high, vaulted ceiling had been much repaired over the years. It made for a grand effect, which worked on Darla, judging by how her jaw dropped. Rory knew that the candles dotting the gathering were not solely for ambience; the ceiling was patched with plaster and looked quite ugly, if functional. More patchwork that the Cat Sidhe had had to pitch together.

Orla led Darla through the hallway into the throne room, fae crowding in front and in her wake. Rory had to nudge and elbow his way through silks and satins, carving a path for himself and Rhiannon, who had to hang onto his jacket tails to stay with the party. As fae reached out to touch Darla's hands and arms, wonder crossed their faces. That would be the energy she exuded, refreshing and revitalising all around her, giving them a jolt they hadn't felt for many years. As Orla moved Darla toward the throne, the crowd thickened, the people in her aura unwilling to stand aside and let go of this feeling.

Introductions passed in a blur, words spoken but no one paying attention to them. All the focus was on Darla, not as herself but as a beacon of pure energy. Rory hovered behind her shoulder, watching the faces pushing in front of her, the hands grasping hers, the lips kissing her palms, a kind of reverence, yes, but a possessive need in each of them. Smiles slipped over the stench of desperation, a thick, cloying sweat that clung to the crowd.

As each new person came forward for a handshake or to kiss her hand or to offer her their arm, Darla greeted them warmly but started to disentangle herself quickly. Each new handshaker clung on for a little too long, their smiles a little too fixed. When one man wrapped his fingers around her wrist, Darla turned her head wildly, her wide eyes meeting Rory's.

Leaning in between Orla and Darla, knocking into his sister's shoulder, he seized the man's arm. "That's enough. Back away."

"But she hasn't met my wife yet. She must meet Catrin!" The Cat Sidhe twisted his arm out of Rory's grip, keeping hold of Darla's hand. He yanked her forward. "This way; it won't be but a moment."

"No." Decorum cast aside, Rory planted himself firmly next to Darla.

The man's lip trembled, looking only at Darla. "My wife, she struggles with her latest babe. Please, it won't take long to meet her."

Darla put a hand to her mouth. "How can I help?"

"Darla," Rory muttered low.

She met his eyes. "I want to be of use, if I can."

Rory's stomach twisted. What was the cost of that? Nothing in this world came for free.

The man's eyes sparked eagerly. "Come."

Rory frowned down at Darla, but she didn't notice; her attention was on the man as he led her through the crowd, away from Orla. Rory walked alongside her, knocking people's hands out of the way as they reached for her skirts.

Chairs had been set out, filled with all manner of the sick and ill. They had tried to put on finery, yes, but dresses hung on stark bones, contrasting sharply with sallow or yellowing skin.

The man tugged Darla toward a heavily pregnant woman, who panted underneath a fur stole. "This is Catrin. Catrin? This is the selkie. She will help you."

"Thank you," the woman mewed. Sweat trickled down her temple.

Darla lifted her hands hesitantly and placed them on the woman's clammy forehead. The woman took in a long deep breath. "That's wonderful. Oh! Simply divine."

Chairs creaked as the sick and the needy leaned toward Darla, some reaching out their arms. Darla bit her lip looking at them, and Rory's cracked heart lurched. There were too many, there had always been too many, but Darla seemed energised, fuelled with purpose. She evidently enjoyed having something meaningful to do. She did not seem taxed by helping these help-less, yet. Rory's arms shook with tension. Yes being the key word.

Darla began moving around the perimeter, and Rory did not leave her side. At some point, Orla must have bade the musicians to play and the food to be served, as strums of string music filtered to his ears and hot scents played around his nose. This did not distract Darla, who focused on the Cat Sidhe who needed her.

Darla spoke to everyone, even those who did not seem to hear. She smiled and laughed at small, cracked voices making small talk. Gazes followed her everywhere, hands trembled as they touched her, and Rory's chest clenched tighter with every new addition to the crowd surrounding them.

Darla's hands wavered. Rory put his arm in her path as she went to speak to the next eager petitioner, a thin man sitting on the edge of his seat. "Wait. Take a moment."

"There's so many to see. I want to meet them all," Darla whispered back. This close, Rory the yellow and red ribbon of her dress clinging to her body, shiny with sweat. The close press of figures, or something else? "Look, I'm actually helping them!"

Rory spared a brief glance for the crowd, but the quiver in her lips, the tightness in her eyes, made his heart falter. "It's drawing from you. You need to be careful, Orla said you wouldn't feel any ill effect, but I'm not so sure. We need to be cautious until we understand more."

"But they look so much better, Rory! I'm making such a difference, and I'm not even doing anything, I'm just being me."

Rory wanted to press her close to his chest, hear his shirt whisper along her bare stomach, put his arms around her and spirit her away. She was strong, yes, and the delight in her face made his heart jump into a gallop, but why strain her?

He searched for an argument to make, hitching a smile into place. "Surely you'd like to enjoy yourself and experience a proper ball for the first time." He lowered his voice, taking her hand in his and pressing it to his chest. "There are many firsts one can experience at a dance such as this."

Her eyes widened slightly, essaying a quick head turn toward the music. Rory's heart leapt. Yes, choose something for yourself. Be selfish for once.

Darla turned back to him with a sigh. "That sounds nice, but I can do some good here. It won't take long. Besides," she laughed, "I don't actually know how to dance."

"I'll teach you," a man called out from behind Rory. "Come with me."

"Me. I'm next!" The old man reached from the chairs, voice quavering.

"I've waited long enough," a woman behind them called. "I followed her all the way in here!"

"I just want a little bit of your time," a fat man said, shouldering his way through.

The woman shoved him away. "Wait your turn!"

"I have a more pressing need!"

Darla raised her hands high in the air. "I do want to meet you all. Please be patient."

"I can pay!" A thin woman held up her jewels in a white-knuckled fist.

The fat man scoffed. "I can pay more than that!"

"Here, you said you wanted to dance." Another man took Darla's hand. "Let me teach you."

The first woman grabbed her other wrist. "It's my turn! She needs to see me first!"

"All of you, stop it!" Rory roared. "Give her some space."

Darla tried to pull her arms in, but the faes held on gamely, glaring at each other over her. The fat man lurched forward, perhaps pushed from behind, and ended up grabbing Darla around her waist. "Ah," the fat man sighed, pressing his head to her stomach.

She reared back. "Let me go!"

With a snarl, Rory dug his nails into the woman's arm and threw it back in her face as she screamed. Punching the face of the would-be dance instructor, he slid beside Darla and kicked the fat man off her. He quickly assessed Darla, holding his arm out for her if she needed to grab on to something. Her pupils were even smaller than ever, and she stood stock still. *Not good.*

"Back off!" Rory's shout rang to the rafters. The music stuttered to a stammering halt. "If any of you lays a hand on her, I will bite it off." Stupid, mindless, greedy fae! "We're leaving."

"You can't have her all to yourself, Rory." Orla glided toward them, Kater behind her right shoulder. Her face was warm with a playful smile in place, but her gaze snapped to Darla and back again to Rory.

Darla looked fine, but Rory knew otherwise. "She's not well, this is too much." Openly defying Orla in front of others was risky, she needed to maintain that she was in control at all times and could make an example of him, but Rory would rather that than hurt Darla.

Orla pouted but inclined her head. "A short break, perhaps. It must be hard to be thrust into the centre of attention from such a backwater life. Literally, in your case, dear."

Rory's bile rose. The crowd might not have let up; Darla could have been torn apart by myopic greed.

He focused on Darla, blocking out the overcrowded room with his body and shielding her from the stares and mutters. "Darla," he whispered, careful that no one else could hear her true name, brushing her forehead to dry the sweat standing there.

Her gaze met his, the spark roaring back behind her eyes. At last.

"This is... this is a lot." She swallowed hard. "I'd like to take a break, please."

"Of course." Rory cupped her face in his hand, wiping the moisture away with his thumb, wishing he could erase the tightness around her jaw as easily. "Is this alright?"

"Yes," she said, her eyes fathomless. Her hand curled around his, her skin far warmer than he had ever felt it. *This cannot be good.*

He put his arm around her back, their steps ringing around the throne room shocked into silence until the Cat Sidhe rumbled, discontented with the energy being taken away. Rory caught the brunt of the glances and glares as whispers started, a rush like the incoming tide in their wake, and Rory fought the urge to pick Darla up and run.

"All in good time," Orla's magically enhanced voice rang out. "Our esteemed guest will be hosted by us for quite a while yet. Please, enjoy tonight's party. Tomorrow's will be even bigger!"

Cheers went up, and Darla slapped her hands over her ears, whimpering. Rory held her closer, pressing her trembling body close to his to shore her up. Orla wouldn't be pleased he was taking Darla away, but Orla could go to the Otherworld.

Rory waved the guards posted at the doors to let them out, keeping a steady hand on Darla's back, and they slid spears back into place to block anyone else from following.

"Wait up!" Rhiannon puffed and panted after them, red faced.

After a heartbeat's hesitation, Rory signalled the guards to let her through. They lifted their spears for Rhiannon to tumble after them, but they barred the crowd beyond. Men and women peered after them, their eyes glittering with loss and hope.

Rhiannon's red face turned out to be from tears. She sniffed and sobbed as Rory quick-marched them back toward the bedrooms. "I lost you in the crowd. They were a bit intense, weren't they?"

"There was nearly a riot." Rory kept his voice level and clear even though he was fuming.

"They... they need help." Darla looked over her shoulder. "That's why they were so insistent. They need help."

Rory shook his head. "They need more than you can give them." One person could not solve their problems. He knew that better than anyone.

"I tried, I... I can get better, I can practice."

Her words squeezed his heart. "No." Rory resisted the urge to crush her to his chest and protect her from all comers, but the threat to her was not in the vicinity; it was the one that menaced the realm, the one that was winning.

He had to keep feeding the Worldheart with souls. The misery of his people, desperate enough to swarm a guest of the queen, spoke to that larger threat. His people needed magic, needed it like air to breathe, and if they weren't to snuff out the smallest spark of it, they needed it in much larger quantities.

Darla made it to her rooms but at the threshold, she wavered. Rory bent, ready to catch her, but she straightened and walked the last few paces to a chair.

Rhiannon interlaced her fingers and stretched them out in front of her. "I've got this, Rory. I don't think there are any injuries, but I've got an emerald just in case."

He hesitated at the doorway. His jacket lay open on the bed, arms wide as if ready for an embrace. Darla stared straight ahead, not looking at him. She was overwhelmed, perhaps frightened, and she might want to go back to her home as soon as she could. Rory's heart wrenched. His people would never let her leave.

"Make sure you put the wards up," he ordered Rhiannon.

The little fae rolled her eyes. "And make sure the bed bugs don't bite, aye." She gave him a cheery wave. "I have an amulet straight to Kater and I won't leave her side. We'll be fine, Rory."

Rory nodded, gaze once again going to Darla. She had slipped her shoes off, tucking her bare feet into the side of the chair, arms around her knees.

I have to fix this.

Rory was halfway down the corridor before he realised he had not said goodbye. It was too late now, and in any case, he would be back before she knew it. The sight of her still and shocked choked him.

Rattling down the stairs two at a time, he rounded the corner just as Orla was making her stately way to her office, her red dress illuminated by flickering candlelight and the ever-present Kater in tow. She had pulled the dried brown fur from the throne over her shoulders, possibly for comfort. Perhaps she took strength from the indestructible thing.

"Orla!" Rory hissed.

She raised her head to look up at him. "Is she well?"

"She's physically fine." His fingers curled around the bannisters. "I need to borrow some magic."

Orla's tipped up face looked odd, upside down like this. Different, as if she were a stranger. "Mm. What for?"

Rory licked his dry lips. "The pelt. You said that would have plenty of energy in it."

Orla's face remained calm, serene, but a small smile trickled onto her face. "Yes, enough and to spare."

Rory's hold on the banister tightened. "And no risk to her? You promise?"

Orla's smile widened. "None. You have my word."

Rory shut his eyes tight. "I'll get changed and go immediately."

Orla's white teeth flashed in the flickering lights, her face stark against the brown fur around her shoulders. "Very good."

CHAPTER 15

Darla

"It's all got a bit much," Rhiannon was saying, running water into a basin. "It's been a big day for you. Why, entering the fae realm two days ago, all the new sights, sounds and smells today, and then that ball." Shaking her head, she brought the steaming bowl closer to set on the floor in front of Darla's chair. "Feet, please."

Darla uncurled slightly, interest piqued by the pleasant smell from the coils of steam. "What's that?"

"Salt bath." Rhiannon grinned at her. "Thought you'd feel a bit more at home."

Darla smiled at the fae's thoughtfulness. She touched a toe to the water. "It's too warm for the sea. The smell is nearly there. Needs more..." She waved her fingers in the air. "Flotsam."

Rhiannon put a hand over her mouth and giggled. Darla did the same, hiding her teeth.

The water was soothing, the warmth relaxing the small muscles in her toes. Muscles she had overused in the last two days, as they were hardly needed as a seal. Everything was so different and yet, somehow, the same.

There was a resource shortage. Darla recognised the dire need in the faces and the actions of the fae downstairs. Shortages happened occasionally to all colonies; despite planning ahead, disaster could strike her colony's winter stores, and hunters could be unlucky too many times. Fortunately, her colony had never been at the brink of destruction, but other desperate colonies had attacked hers before. When a colony was devastated enough to try to take another, it was a fight to the death.

The Cat Sidhe had likely made the logical connection: If there was one selkie, there were bound to be others. Would the Cat Sidhe want her to contact her colony? To persuade them to help, maybe? Would they try to take them? Her chest felt tight at the idea, too large to be acknowledged.

No, Rory, Rhiannon, the fae she had met had all acted kindly toward her. She had to focus on their similarities rather than what set them apart. She clearly recalled Rory's sudden dart toward her and his strong form wrapping around her. Her core tingled. He would not let harm come to her. He had confronted his matriarch, and she had not struck him down but let her leave. The colony here was struggling, but it had not stripped down the vestiges of civilisation to survive just yet. Darla would provide what help she could as thanks to her hosts, and then be on her way.

Sighing, she pulled her feet from the basin and dried them on a nearby towel, soft as the clam inside its shell. "Thank you. I do feel better."

Rhiannon sat on the edge of the bed. "You want to talk about it? Oh, I ordered food sent up, by the way."

Darla sat next to her, untying the ribbons around her neck. "I think I see the scale of the problem now. Do *you* want to talk about it?"

"Eh?" Rhiannon cocked her head.

Patting her friend's arm, Darla started pulling the ribbons

free. "About what's happening here. I want to hear from you about the magic draining from the land and what it's doing to your people."

"Oh. That." Rhiannon's back slumped. "Well, it's hard. I try to help as many people as I can, but it's getting harder for me to get enough to charge my emeralds, and without them, I can't help anyone. It's like... pushing a boulder uphill, and if I stop, it'll roll to the bottom again. But instead of making me, like, super fit, it's just tiring me out from having to do it all the time." Rhiannon closed her eyes briefly. "Sorry. It's not something we usually trot out in front of guests."

"That's alright, I did ask." Darla struggled as a knot of ribbons tangled in her hair. Rhiannon sat up to help, gently parting her curls to find the offending clump. "It's real and it needs dealing with."

"We are, except nothing seems to work. We lose every time we skirmish with the Cu Sidhe, blasted dogs." Rhiannon teased the knot apart, her hands gentle despite the frustration in her voice. "Rory is hardly ever here. He's constantly throwing himself against it, securing as many souls as he can. He works alone because he says he does better that way, but I think it's because he couldn't bear to lose anyone." Her hands dropped into her lap. "There."

Rory was a hunter, then, pulling back resources that his people needed and daring against death every day. He had been unconscious when she found him. How often did he drive himself to the brink like that? The scars on his well-worked hands were endless. How long had he been fighting to push away the threat to his colony?

Did he ever ask for help?

Darla pulled her hair free. "Finally, thank you."

"Yeah, good job you didn't get into a compromising situation, that would have ruined the moment." Rhiannon passed her a soft t-shirt.

Darla held it up. "Bite me," she read.

"Yeah. Thought you'd like that. Rory said you'd like it, and he told me how you dealt with the redcaps." Rhiannon chuckled. "Can't believe you didn't get sick after chomping on one of them."

Darla pulled it over her head, standing up to remove the skirt of the lovely dress. "Those fae downstairs very nearly did eat me, didn't they?" She had not truly appreciated how at risk she had been, as the crowd had built slowly but steadily. Rory had sensed the danger from his own people and stuck by her side. He knew how desperate they were.

Rhiannon's face fell. "Oh, sorry, yes. I'll get a different one, I'm such an idiot."

"You're not an idiot." Darla let her hands fall. "They were scared for themselves but mostly for others. And I did help. Did you see some of the people afterwards? One man had no idea where he was, but I took his hand and he focused on me. Then he turned to the woman next to me and said, "Julia!" and she started crying. She was his daughter, and he hadn't recognised her for months, she said."

Rhiannon put her hands on her hips. "Yes, but don't forget, we all have to fade at some point. Death is a natural part of all life."

Darla waved a hand. "I know that. But losing even one being before their time is a huge blow, that wealth of knowledge lost, that potential gone."

They were quiet for a time, each swimming in their own thoughts. Rhiannon got into the bed, holding out the covers for Darla. It was nice to share warmth and snuggle close with someone, but Rhiannon did not smell like Neri. A wave of longing for the sea and her sister slammed into Darla; tears pearled in her eyes. Rhiannon said nothing, gently stroked her shoulders, humming a little tune as Darla sobbed briefly.

Recovering, Darla rubbed her eyes. "Thank you."

Rhiannon nodded slowly. "It's what I do."

Darla's worries would feel lesser when shared, she knew, and perhaps Rhiannon could help her assuage her worry-born fears. "Rhiannon, is Orla... a good matriarch?"

She cocked her head. "You mean a good queen? Yes, I suppose she is. Took over from her mother. Orla can be caring, sometimes, but... Well." Rhiannon cleared her throat. "Some say she's ruthless."

A pang raced through Darla. "She does what needs to be done? No matter the cost?"

Rhiannon's curls bounced as she nodded. "No matter the cost to her or Kade or Rory. And sometimes... others."

Rhiannon's grip on her hand felt too tight now. Darla squirmed a little, but she did not notice, letting out a low sigh.

"Did you know there's a saying? Never trust a Cat Sidhe. Maybe I should put that on a t-shirt." Rhiannon's face hardened, her eyes unfocused.

She had to be careful, and set out clear boundaries for helping. Rory wouldn't take more than she could give.

Darla startled when a rapping sound rang from the door.

"Hey, food is here, good timing." Rhiannon wriggled out of bed to open the door, animated once more. "I got one of everything."

Fae set the platters on tables, shooting glances at Darla as they left. Darla squirmed in the bedsheets, the attention suddenly too much. The food they left smelled good, her stomach aching with hunger, but a deeper ache took hold.

"I want to help Rory help you," she whispered to Rhiannon.

She cheerfully took a bite of some kind of meat, passing the rest to Darla. "One step at a time."

CHAPTER 16

Rory

Rory's eyes stung from salt and sand and the brutal wind whipping it into his face. It did not deter him. Stretching out his soul sense, Rory felt a strong pull toward one area of the beach, down by the tideline. Sticks and bottles lay washed up amongst smoothed pebbles, the sand dense and dark, potent with water under his feet.

Rory walked on until his senses jangled, coming up to a collection of energy so unimaginably vast, it set his teeth on edge.

"Your Highness?" Kater held a shovel in both hands across his huge body. He could easily use it as a weapon.

Rory had not wanted Kater along, but Orla had insisted. "Just in case the Cu Sidhe are there, hunting the pelt," she had said, giving them copious magic, but there was likely another reason: In case he decided not to go through with it.

What Orla did not appreciate was that Rory's course was set. Darla would not be able to help all his people on her own, he knew that. One person could not change this tide, and throwing himself at it endlessly had nearly killed him, both in body and in spirit. He did not want that fate for Darla, because of course she would want to help. He saw it in her eyes, the hope and wonder, the realisation that she could do something meaningful for his people.

Rory did not want the hope that had died in him to flicker out in Darla.

The grit stuck in Rory's throat. "Here." He pointed to an unremarkable stretch of sand.

Kater started digging, depositing massive piles of sand with each heave of the spade, his exertions as methodical as a machine. He did not have to dig long before the spade came up with a dangling shape cascading over it.

It looked like someone had buried a very thin rug. Underneath the clinging tan sand, the fur was brown and grey. It pumped out massive amounts of potential, so much so that to Rory the air above it wavered. Bile rose in his throat as Kater laid the skin to one side of the hole he had dug. "We are lucky, Your Highness."

"Lucky?"

"Yes. Even I can feel the energy pouring from this, and I have no soul-sense to speak of. I wondered whether the Cu Sidhe would be all over this." He flexed his arms, one half of the big man's face looking pensive beside the silver mask. "She is lucky she ran into you and not the Cu Sidhe."

Rory's chest tightened further. The Cu Sidhe escorted souls to vanish into the Otherworld. Darla was clearly living, but would they have made a distinction for her pelt?

Using the edge of the spade, Kater folded the skin in half and half again, then slid the spade under to lift it into his bag. "Good, our work here is complete."

Rory snatched the bag up, pulling it to his chest, before Kater could take it. The fae's eyes glittered briefly, then subsided with a smile.

Leaving the spade and the hole, the two fae walked along the shoreline, heading for the copse of trees that came close to the water's edge and afforded some cover. With each step away from the fur's hiding place, sensation trickling across Rory's own skin. He scanned the waves greedily lapping the sand and the empty horizon, but he still couldn't shake the sense that someone or something glared accusingly at him.

"We are secure here. We can make a tear to create a bridge across." Kater gestured to Rory.

"Right, yes." Lifting his hand, Rory made a start. He didn't have to touch the magic Orla had afforded him; the emanations from the fur were more than enough, sending sparks shooting up his arms as he tried to control the raw magic lashing around him.

Swearing, Rory pulled them through, staggering from the sheer force of it.

He jumped when Kater patted him on the back. "Excellent. I will wash this and then take it to the Worldheart. The queen is no doubt waiting for a report from you."

"She is, but I'm not leaving that pelt until I see it secured." Rory's throat closed. Was bringing the pelt here the right thing to do? "Tell Orla I am going to the tether."

Kater inclined his head, and Rory turned on his heel, trying not to feel like an asshole. The Cu Sidhe would have found it and taken it if he had not, surely?

What if Darla could sense it? If she did, then what could he say? Option one was to say he wrestled it from some kind of enemy. Maybe the redcaps they'd met. Yes. He'd appear to be a hero rather than a shitty thief. Option two... Kater could take the heat. Rory could blame it all on him, Orla would go along with it and order Kater to shut up about it. He was pretty sure Orla kept him in the dungeons anyway, but the less he wondered about his sister's habits in that arena, the better.

Option three was to tell the truth. If she found out. Orla was sure she wouldn't be able to sense anything, had given her word that using her pelt would not harm her.

At the edge of the castle was a tower. It too was tumble-down, with missing steps that gaped like teeth. An artery of the Worldheart passed directly underneath and Rory was forever here, depositing the meager scraps of souls he could scrape together.

Rory unlocked the door, setting the bolts back with a clank. Inside was a gleaming structure of iron and thistle, multiple pipes twisting out like tortured branches. It's roots reached right down to a lesser-known stream of the Worldheart. A tether to the Worldheart. As Rory neared it, the tether pulsed with dim silver light.

No one knew who had built it or how many of these there were, and the Cu Sidhe destroyed any that they found. The branches stood only a little taller than Rory. He could hang the pelt like he hung the souls onto it, except this was thick and fine compared to the thin tissue-like quality of individual souls. Each soul caused the branch to pulse, light travelling down to the trunk as if the tether was drinking it down. After a time, one of the buds would ripen and out would pop some small, concentrated pellets of magic, if they were lucky.

Shivering, Rory stepped back, the idea of stretching out the silky pelt to hang sickening him. But the tether flared brightly, light pulsing down from the tips of every single branch. Rory's heart pounded as every single branch burgeoned, fat and ripe, splitting and bursting with collected magic, and the marbles of concentrated magic rolled over the floor, more dropping down with heavy clinks.

"That is the power of a selkie's pelt," Orla said behind Rory.

He wrapped his arms around the bag. "Why? How?"

"Does it matter? We can *breathe*, Rory. We can finally rest, recoup, and we can finally heal." Her hand sought his, squeezed it in hers and then kissed his knuckles, tears in her eyes as she watched the tether. "It will give us the time and energy to figure out how to defeat the Cu Sidhe at long last."

"And it will let Darla explore unmolested, right? When the Cat Sidhe can get their magic from the land again, this wouldn't be necessary. Using the pelt is a stop gap only." He should have asked her, but what if she had said no? Orla would have had no choice but to take it anyway.

He clutched the bag to his chest. "You're sure she cannot feel this? That she won't be affected by it?"

Orla stared at the marbles, blooming and tumbling onto the ground with steady taps. "I am sure."

"How can you be sure?"

Orla bent, picking up a marble. She drew in a slow breath as she absorbed the magic into her palm, the lines on her face easing. "Mother told me."

Mother had met a selkie? That sat uneasily in his mind. "And?"

"And it sustained the realm for decades." Orla's eyes glowed.

"What happened to the selkie?"

Orla rolled her eyes. "Returned to the seas, most likely. They don't like to be away from their waters for long." She hastily banished the smile from her face. "I can tell this is hard on you. Really, it's for the best. A tough decision well made."

Rory felt sick, but he had to stick to the best of the bad options he had been presented with. "Where can we put this so it's safe?" The idea of draping it on the branches felt too much like hanging Darla up there.

Orla gestured to a cabinet set to one side. "I had something brought from the human realm. Bullet proof glass, they call it, a substance which cannot be smashed."

Rory put the bag inside. It slumped over, and Rory righted it, thinking of the pelt compressed inside. His hands left the straps slowly, fingers unpeeling one after the other.

Orla shut and locked the pane, putting the key on her necklace. "Wonderful. Let's return to the castle." Stooping, Orla picked up handfuls of magic, smiling at Rory. She looked decades younger, a ringlet escaping from her severe bun. "Here. Take some. Take as many as you like."

Rory held out his hand. The marbles felt heavy in his hand. Dense and rich.

He closed his eyes, thrusting back the surge of sickness that threatened to close his throat. This would sustain his realm until Orla could defeat the Cu Sidhe. Repeating that to himself as he entered the castle, he shunned any eye contact with the early morning risers and servants that littered the halls. The party seemed to have gone on all night, with even a few intrepid fae still propping up the bar.

Rory dug his nails into his palms, welcoming the sharp grounding from pinpricks of pain. "Hurry up and defeat Shay."

"Oh, Rory. We all have to do what we can. Your work now is simple and fun." She ventured a smile. "Make her want to stay for as long as possible while I rest up. That should be easy if you show her everything she wants to see. She has quite the list and... I hesitate in saying this, but she had some nascent feelings for you, you know. They came through loud and clear when we met, and last night again. It's adorable."

Rory's stomach twisted hard, as if Orla had strung out his guts to use as violin strings. He said nothing, but inside, that treacherous spark flickered against his heart. His chest swelled. Damn Orla, for knowing which of his buttons to push.

She touched his cheek. "You could make her want to stay all on your own, my pretty brother. Who knows? Perhaps this will be the making of you as well. You'll finally settle down."

That hope also seared into him. How could he bring children into this world to face challenges he had no hope of defeating himself? But now, with the end in sight...

Enabled with just a little deception. A small theft, in the grand scheme of things. They could laugh about this on their honeymoon, how he stole her skin to keep her, just as the legends say; a Cat Sidhe cannot resist a soul for their own purposes, and selkies are kept bound to the one who has their skin...

Orla ruffled his hair gently. "Get some rest. The day is young yet, but already I can feel—-"

A clatter rang down the staircase, and Rory leapt in front of Orla, arms raised ready to defend. Rhiannon stood on the stairs, chest heaving. "Something's changed, I can feel the magic again. Is it returning?"

Orla glanced at Rory. "We have had an exceptional haul."

"Is Darla alright?" Rory demanded.

His heartrate spiked when Rhiannon shook her head. "Oh, she was all sorts of upset yesterday. She's probably still sleeping now, I left her in the early hours to do my rounds with my patients, and—"

Rory resisted the urge to shake her. The fae had done nothing wrong. "But she's physically well? Guarded?"

"Yes? The usual wards are up." She frowned, looking between the siblings. "Is this extra magic because she's been here for a few days now?"

"No," Orla said smoothly. Another lie told through a partial truth. "We have bought ourselves some significant time, and so now is our chance to seize the moment and strike at the dogs. We have magic enough and to spare, and none of our elderly need perish because our fighters need more fuel."

Rhiannon nodded, wide eyed, admiration and awe dawning in her face. Rory wished he could be easily swayed by Orla's leadership, her stirring slogans and passion for her people. All he felt was the cost.

But it was different now. He could rest for a while. He had earned it.

Rory nodded to Rhiannon, bowed to Orla. "I'm going to check on Darla. Good night. Morning. Whatever."

"Good work, Rory," Orla purred as he sprinted up the stairs.

It wasn't over, not yet, but just feeling how different the air felt... it didn't smell or even taste different, it didn't sound any different, but Rory's heart felt lighter than it had for years. It had been weighted down ever since Orla had come to him, telling him it was his responsibility to help, that she couldn't do it alone and needed help shouldering the burden. Rory would have the rest of his life to figure out what next for him.

Taking the stairs two at a time, Rory walked down the corridor. Darla's room was the next one on the left. He slowed. Could he just knock the door, pretend he was just passing? He *was* just passing; that wasn't a falsehood. Why were his palms sweating over knocking on a door?

Rory recognized his feelings of attraction for what they were, welcoming them. He was head over heels in lust, not guilty. Not at all.

He knocked on the door, both excited and anxious for her to open it. He waited.

She didn't answer it.

He knocked again, a little louder. "It's me. Rory."

Still nothing. No movement inside the room either.

Rory disabled the wards with a few words. They unravelled quickly, magic more responsive than he could recall it being for many years. He cracked open the doorway and peered in. In the centre of a bunched bundle lay Darla. One of her long legs wrapped around the duvet, holding it close to her. Something dark red pooled under her head, the colour of dried blood. He rushed to the bed. *No.* No, no, no...

She inhaled, sleeping atop of his dark red jacket. His heart panged even as relief swept into him, releasing his tight chest. She was deeply asleep, as Rhiannon said, and he would come back later when she was awake.

Still, he stole a quick moment of peace, listening to her rhythmic breathing. Smudges of last night's makeup made tracks where tears had rolled down her cheeks. A powerful urge to wipe those stains away, to erase her heartache, welled in his chest.

"Rory?" Darla struggled upright, rubbing her eyes. "I thought it was you."

"Sorry to disturb…" His gaze dropped to her chest. "'Eat me.' So you like it, then?"

"Mm?" Darla's eyes, the pupils larger in the half light of dawn, followed his gaze. "Oh, yes. Rhiannon finds a lot of these in the closet."

"Yes. I had them put there." Even rumpled from sleep she looked delectable. Eat me, indeed. Through heroic will Rory tamped down the urge to flirt, opening the curtains wide to welcome the sun.

She shielded her eyes from the sudden light. Her shoulders slumped, fingers twining in her lap.

Rory frowned. "Are you alright?"

"I think so, I just need a moment."

"Of course. I didn't mean to intrude. I was checking on you." The dark shadows under her eyes scared him. Yesterday must have drained her hard. "Take all the time you need."

He caught a flash of movement, himself in the mirror. He had a bewildered look in his eyes, but they were bright and, dare he say it, merry. And that after pulling an all-nighter.

Wiping his hands on his jeans, hoping he didn't drop any incriminating sand on the floor, he cleared his throat. "If you're not feeling well, I'll make you breakfast and bring it here for you."

She had her head in her hands.

Rory's mouth dried. "Darla?"

"I don't feel… good. Normal." She hugged her knees, drawing in a long breath. "It's strange. I miss the sea."

He did not dare to approach the bed. He had to leave and change and wash, quickly, get any lingering scent off him. "Do you?" He bit his tongue. Was that the best he could do? "Well, perhaps we can go to the limestone shore. If you're feeling better later, that is." He pretended to look out the window, studying her reflection in the glass. "We could go see the waterfalls of the Fire lands of the realm. They are quite stunning, so high that by the time the water reaches the bottom, it's just mist." Her face would be a picture of wonder, glistening with droplets. "Near there are the obsidian mines, they've been thoroughly dug out and now they are caves, so dark you can't tell which way you're facing." She would probably need to hold hands in there. He rubbed his hands together. "Or there's these fields the flower fae keep, just rows upon rows of all kinds of colours." She would want to study every single flower, gaze intent and focused.

Her reflection stretched back out on the bed. "Maybe." She tucked the jacket under her head, fingers clinging to it. She didn't seem to realise she held it, and the sight hurt Rory's heart just as much as it lifted it. "I think it did wear me out, helping people last night."

His heart lurched. Yes. That's what this was. She was tired from directly helping people with her own energy. It couldn't be anything to do with the pelt. Orla promised. It was for the greater good, and for her benefit. The visiting had tired her out, badly. It was the best option because everyone wins.

Even him. He got to win, for once.

Rory turned around to face the room. "Then rest. You've got a few more days, so I'm going to make you something... special." Yes. She deserved a special treat, and he was going to be the one to wipe all her troubling thoughts away and replace them with pure sensation. A taste sensation to start, and once he had tantalised her taste buds, he would hopefully get to taste her. He could rediscover what fun truly felt like, reinvigorate his carefree days, and the first thing that came to mind was Darla's lips, parted, the straw of the chocolate milkshake between them, and the sheer ecstasy on her face. How many times could he provoke that look? Whether by landscapes or mechanical marvels or the courts of the realm, or, if she welcomed it, with his tongue?

Now that sounds like fun.

His smile widened. "I'll be back later. Get ready for a surprise."

CHAPTER 17
Darla

The twist of delicious anticipation over the surprise that Rory was planning was quickly dampened. A longing for the sea and her sister, as aching as a fresh wound, speared into her. She pushed the thought down. She was a little homesick, that was all. It was to be expected. She had hoped she would be too busy to be homesick, but even though she only had a few days left, she had some stupid desire to go back immediately.

She couldn't let the opportunity slip away. Hunkering lower into Rory's jacket, she breathed in his scent. He had seemed giddy with excitement, and she loved seeing it.

Determined to enjoy the present, Darla forced herself up. The wardrobe doors seemed heavier than usual, and raising her arms above shoulder level caused her muscles to ache. Grabbing the nearest clothes to hand, Darla pulled them on, legs shaking as she fed them into the fabric tubes, fingers tingling with pinpricks of pain as she buttoned them up. She pulled a crop top on, peering at it in the mirror, squinting with the effort of trying to read what it said.

"Oh. It's backwards," she muttered. "Reflection." Her

throat hurt as she swallowed, as if little barnacles had grown in there overnight. *Maybe I've fallen ill?* This was a new realm with lots of new people. Selkies could get ill after mixing with new selkies from other colonies, but they shook disease off quickly.

Darla curled back into the bed, tucking around Rory's jacket. *I'll just rest for a moment.*

Shortly after closing her eyes, a warm hand touched her shoulder. "Darla?"

"Mm?" Her eyelids were heavy. She fought hard to open them. There was so much to see and experience, so much she wanted to do. It wasn't time to sleep for so long and so late.

"Darla." Rory's voice. Soft and inviting. The bed tipped slightly with his weight as he sat next to her. Warmth brushed her ears. "I've got you chocolate."

Chocolate.

Chocolate.

"Chocolate?" Darla opened her eyes.

Rory sat next to her head. He chuckled as she sat upright, offering his arm for her to claw her way up. His smell was so much more vital up close, filled with a heat that the jacket merely shadowed.

He also smelled of something else. Something sweet and bitter at the same time.

Darla looked around. "Where is it?"

His laughter rang around the room. "Come on, I'll take you there." His smile faded. "Can you walk?"

"Yes, yes, of course." Darla swung her legs to the floor and stood up. "See? Fine..." Black spots swarmed her vision. "Uh?"

She clung to Rory's hand as the dancing shapes faded. He touched her upper arm, warm and close. "Are you sure you're able to walk? It's not far; I can carry you."

Her gaze cleared, and his red marbled eyes filled her vision. He had ducked down so their faces were level, and his nose was very close, and under his nose were his lips, and they were right there…

She dragged her eyes back to his. "Pardon?"

Those lips tipped up on one side. "Never mind. We can stay like this if you like." His hand slid up her arm. A shiver raced from the trail of his rough palm up to her neck, a flush of warmth in its wake.

"Rory," she whispered.

His eyes were dark. "Darla." He took a step closer. Shoulders filled her peripheral vision, his arms wrapping around her. Her heart pounded, her lungs tight, but not in a bad way. Her stomach flipped, and then far too many sensations to really get hold of rushed past her; tightness in her chest before a dive, the aching waiting to come to shore, the lightness of finally unfurling into her new body. She wanted to capture them in the photographs she'd heard of, to study this in depth and as many times as she could.

What would happen if she put her hands on his hips? She slid her hands along the hard planes of underneath his skin, rougher compared to hers, more weathered. He made a noise in the back of his throat.

She tipped her head back, studying his lips, and Rory's arms pulled her closer, tightening, and her sped heart even faster. It didn't feel like exertion, this felt like…

Coming home.

His lips were warm against hers, the softest skin, yielding as if they melted against her own, melding and forming a bridge between her being and his. The taste of salt, comforting in its familiarity but exciting in its novelty. *I didn't think he would taste of the sea.*

His hands cradled her head, arms supporting her shoulders as he took her in his arms. Black spots danced in her vision again, but this time it was part of the experience, this light-headedness combined with being grounded and held. His mouth parted and he was the seeker, gently questing forward, his tongue tracing the seam of her lips. Opening for him, she exhaled, her throat tight and chest throbbing as his mouth claimed hers.

His body surged forward like the swell of the waves, sweeping her away. They tumbled onto the bed, the kiss broken as Darla's head sank into the covers. He lay over her, arms trembling and eyes darting between hers. His thin shirt billowed downward, and her gaze traced his rapidly working throat down to the tangle of wet hair on his chest.

She wrapped her arms around his neck, and he collapsed against her with a grin, covering her.

"Darla." His voice was muffled, head pressed between her breasts. He could probably hear her heart, galloping like one of those horses. His weight was solid, real, his body hard against hers. She ran her fingers through his hair. "It feels like I've been wanting to do that for days." What else could she do? How else did he respond when touched by her?

He lifted up on his elbows, smiling down at her. "Me too. I haven't ever felt this way." His eyes were earnest, and Darla stole her hands up his back to his head. The wet red strands of his hair slid through her fingers as she drew his face toward her own. His eyes went darker again and a thrill pebbled her skin as their lips brushed...

Her stomach snarled at him, and a bolt of fear shot through her. She slapped her hands to her mouth. "I'm not making that noise on purpose!" What if he thought that was a warning noise or something? "I'm not growling at you!"

Fortunately, he threw his head back and laughed. "Come." Rory's eyes were still dark, tempered with a glittering amusement. "You're hungry. I'm hungry too, but I can wait." He licked his lips, and the sight of his questing pink tongue made Darla's core tremble. "Let's get some food in you. You need to replenish your energy, and store some up for later." He winked at her.

"Later? Are there other people that need help? I didn't get them all yesterday."

Something like anger flickered in his face as he helped her upright, a determined set to his jaw. "No, you did enough yesterday. There's been... something of a development." He looked away. "Magic has returned for now. Can you feel it?"

"What? Returned how? I can't feel anything." Well, nothing but the strange lack of energy, a current downwards as if she were caught in the edge of a riptide and being slowly dragged down to the seafloor. The kiss had helped, even if only distracting her from her homesickness.

He took her hand, his scent ttingling the spot where her whiskers should be. Soon, maybe they would smell the same, a shared colony-scent of their very own. A pairing.

She tipped her face up for another taste, but his eyes were sad. He should be delighted that the magic had returned. "Rory?"

"I..." His fingers intertwined with hers, thumbs rubbing the back of her hands. "You're so much colder than usual."

"Am I? I feel very warm." She shivered as his thumbs brushed her skin. *Maybe I am a little cold.*

"Let's get some nourishment in you, although I fear this is more a feast for the soul than nutrients for the body." He winced at his words. Why was that? "Calories are calories, and you need a lot. Come."

Hand in hand they walked down the corridor. Rory was silent, thrumming with tension. Could it be worry? What was he worried about, now that magic had returned?

"You must be so relieved about the magic coming back," she said.

His eyes closed briefly. "Yes," he responded in monotone.

The joy had drained from him again, his movements stiff and tortured compared to the ease of earlier.

She drew to a halt. "What's the matter?"

His gaze dropped to the floor. "I'm worried about you."

"About me?" Darla's cheeks stretched into a smile. "I'll be alright. I'm just tired."

"Yes." Putting his arm around her shoulders, he tucked her close to his side. It was strange to walk like that, to accommodate the strides of another person, but they managed it together, their bodies responding to one another.

He steered her toward the throne room, and her stomach tightened, recalling the press and crush of bodies from last night. A big seat Darla had not noticed last time dominated the far end, drawing Darla's attention as a strange chill settled over her. She jerked to a halt. Something was wrong with that chair.

Rory had halted at the same time she had, following her rapt attention. "That's Orla's throne. Queen of the Cat Sidhe needs a bit of ostentation to it."

"Yes." Darla bit her lip. Something about that throne called to her, as if someone in need cried out hopelessly. *It's too late to help*. The feeling faded as quickly as it had laid over her. Shaking her head, she clung on to Rory's hand. "I... I think I need to eat something."

"Right away. I can't wait to see your face." Putting his hand on the small wooden side door, he looked back over his shoulder. His figure made her mouth run dry, all hard planes and broad shoulders underneath the thin shirt, but it was his smile that made her heart leap. His drying hair was tousled, eyes dancing, face flushed. He was excited, and that excitement lifted her own heart.

He shoved the door open.

Inside was a set of tables laid out in a horseshoe shape. Walking in a daze to stand in the middle, Darla was surrounded on three sides with an array of all shades and shapes of brown.

There were milkshakes, yes, but these were topped with a heavy swirl of cream, decorated with shavings. The bitter smell of warm chocolate rose from several sticky rectangles, dripping with some kind of glaze. There was a cake topped with pecans and coconuts, and some kind of fluffy pillow that had melted.

"Marshmallows." Taking a fork, Rory speared one. "Try it?"

He guided it to her mouth, and the taste was pure sugar sweetness. Darla gasped. The marshmallow was warm and slid over her tongue delightfully.

"There's some in here too. S'mores volcanos." He held up something sandwiched between two biscuits, dripping with brown sauce. He winced a little as some seeped onto his skin. "That's hot."

Darla took his hand and laid her tongue along the edge of his thumb. The offending sauce was indeed hot, and delicious.

Rory's eyes were dark. "Very hot."

Darla looked around. There was so much more! "What's this? And this?"

"Let me remember. I only eat the desserts; I don't know what half the stuff is called." He pointed at the pecan coconut cake. "Mississippi mud cake." To the rectangles. "Bourbon brownies."

Darla gasped. "Actual *brownies*?"

Rory snorted. "No, that's just a name for cake." He slid his arm around her. "I wouldn't feed you fae, Darla darling."

It was the second time he had called her that, but this time she could tell a weight of sentiment waited behind the words. Watching his face, her chest seemed to glow at his enthusiasm.

He pointed to another large cake. "Groom's cake with brownie pieces and fudge." To a pan of other, darker brownies. "Death by chocolate."

Darla eyed it. "Oh. That one sounds rather final."

"It's just a name. Try some."

Taking a spoon, Darla dipped it into the pan. The top had a resistance to it, then it gave willingly, and the smell very nearly overwhelmed her. The taste was something else again; hard and soft, achingly sweet with an edge.

"Well? What do you think?" Rory came to stand next to her.

Darla leaned her hip into him, finger trembling. "How did you make all this?"

Rory laughed. "I didn't make it. I explored all the way around the human realm. But don't worry, I..." He swallowed, hard. "I paid fair money for these."

Staring at the chocolate decadence surrounding her, Darla paused. Magic had been so rare here, people were dying. But now there was a glut of it. Surely, it was alright to use some for something else.

"Here, try this," Rory said, lifting up yet another brownie. "Brownie surprise. Layered with peanut butter." That gave a crunch like bashed barnacles, which Darla loved. "Chocolate sponge with Nutella." Darla's thoughts were swirled away in a ganache that tasted like nuts and frosting. "Oh, black forest cake." This one was darker yet, nearly as black as the selkie matriarch, lined with neat chocolate chips and perfect red round fruits that burst between Darla's lips.

"Steady on." Rory laughed as she staggered.

She bumped into the milkshake, holding it still. Taking a swipe of the cream, she laid it on his nose. He let her, eyes dancing, and then mock growled and grabbed her around the waist. "You'll pay for that."

"Oh, the scary Cat Sidhe." She grinned, grabbing a handful of his hair and gently tipping his head to the side. His pulse jumped in his throat, a combination of overpowered yet able to move at any time. He was putting control over his body in her hands, and that was as intoxicating as a river of chocolate.

A rich dark chocolate fountain flowed next to a molten chocolate pudding with coconut cream on top. It was all so much, dizzying and overwhelming, but in the best way. Like Rory's kisses.

She held up the bowl that the hot cake resided in. "How do you eat this?"

Rory held up a spoon. "I can feed you, if you'd like."

The edge of the spoon cut into the cake, dipping and then parting. He lifted the spoon, hovering a hand underneath to catch unruly drips of runny chocolate sauce.

Darla enveloped it all, the sweetness exploding in her mouth, and she moaned with pleasure.

"Oh, fae gods," Rory muttered. "This is even better than I thought it would be."

Pulling the spoon out of her mouth, she gave it a long languorous lick it. Rory groaned, clutching her hips. She went on her tiptoes, and he pressed his lips to hers as if hungry for more than chocolate.

Their kiss seemed to exist outside of time, a slow deep communion of her body to his. His lips stroked hers, sending a

When she broke off, he was panting. Smears of chocolate lined his swollen lips, smudges on his jaw and in his hair where her hands had roamed. Her own mouth was teased to throbbing.

"Darla." Her name on his lips wrapped around her like magic, binding her to him. "There's so much I want to do with you. To you, to some extent, but mostly with you." He squeezed her hand tight, leaning down to whisper in her ear, "We can take our time. Let's take this slow."

Bitter seawater flooded her mouth, but she consoled herself. She could enjoy and catalogue these moments, and prepare to savour many, many more before she had to return in a few days. "Alright then."

He pressed a chaste closed-mouth kiss to her cheek, still thrilling but miles behind the open-mouthed embrace where she half thought she would be eaten, and gestured to the treats. "We have barely begun."

They sampled the nutty brownies and luscious pieces of

banana, fed each other cherries, chocolate staining their finger-tips. Tart juice burst on her lips. Darla's stomach soon became fuller than her heart, but something niggled at her. Her gaze kept landing on the small door to the cavernous throne room beyond.

"I can lock the door if that's what you're worried about. No one will disturb us." Rory ran his fingers up her arms to her shoulders. "Or we can give them a show."

Her core warmed, but quickly chilled. "No, I... Sorry. There's something strange out there."

"Oh?" His eyes slid away. "Maybe you're feeling the magic returning. The air does feel different."

Darla shifted a brownie aside, shimmying her backside onto the table. "How did the magic return? What happened? Are souls being returned to the land by the Cu Sidhe now?"

"Not yet, but once we defeat them, that is what we will do. Then it will always be like this." He sat next to her, but his smile was pasted on as surely as the cakes had been piled with decadent icing.

Darla's cheeks tingled, Rhiannon's warning coming unbidden: *Never trust a Cat Sidhe.* She rubbed her face, but while Rory's words hadn't been a lie, there was something he wasn't telling her.

"Rory, how has the magic been restored?"

He bit his lower lip. "Can we talk about something else first? We still have time to go to the flower fae fields if you'd like—"

She took his head in her chocolate covered hands, palms to his cheeks. "Rory. The lack of magic here was a huge issue. Everyone was hiding how scared they were. How did it resolve practically overnight?"

He couldn't hold her gaze, and a flare flashed in Darla's bloated belly. "Rory, what aren't you telling me?"

"I... I'm trying to find the words." His eyes swam with tears.

"Darla, let's stay here. Let's just eat more chocolate, and kiss, and I'll make love to you all the ways that you want, even ways you've never dreamed of." He leaned forward to kiss her.

Darla reared back. "What is it? What have you done?" Unease swamped her like a cold current in warm seas.

Rory hands darted out for her.

She evaded his grasp, slipping between the tables, and crashed into the door. It flung open with a loud bang that rang up to the rafters of the huge hall.

Darla dashed to the throne, toward that small pull, the echo of a cry long since silenced. Her footsteps pounded in time with her heart and her chest clamped too tight for her to breathe.

Draped across the throne of dry bones was a tan hide, so drained it was limp and thin. The mummified fur resembled marram grass along the coast rather than the rich silky chocolate brown it should have been.

Darla's heart thumped with every slow step she took up to the throne. No. No, it couldn't be.

The rattle of Rory's steps halted just behind her. She whirled around, fists raised and teeth bared.

He held up his empty hands. "Darla, I can explain. I will explain. Please, just listen—"

She thrust a finger at the pelt. "Explain *that*? How will you ever be able to justify that poor selkie's skin to me?"

Rory frowned at the fur, then turned a beseeching look to her. It tore at her heart. "What do you mean? That's some old fur my mother had, it's always on the throne. Orla wears it occasionally." Truth rang in his words.

"It's a selkie's pelt." Her shoulders shook. "It doesn't belong here. Whose is it?"

His chocolate smeared mouth dropped open, shock widening his eyes, but it could all be lies. Never trust a Cat Sidhe.

"A selkie…" He gasped, as if all the air had been punched out of him. "A selkie's! Darla, I didn't know!"

Darla stumbled backward, wavering hands gathering the fur. The poor thing, who knew what kind of fate the wild fae had met here, in the halls of the lying Cat Sidhe? She gathered it to her chest, but was that to protect it or to comfort herself?

Her voice trembled. "The magic that's back, that came from me, didn't it? But I don't have enough to power a whole land! I was so drained after last night…" Her fingers buried deep into the fur. No. It couldn't be.

Rory's hands flexed, his gaze hard. "Last night drained you badly, but you would have gladly thrown yourself at it again. You wanted to help people, but you can't help this, and they would have taken everything, all your vibrance, all your happiness." Tears rolled down his cheeks. "They would have drained you of your life, Darla. Please, you have to understand. I had no other option."

The fur trembled in her hands. "You took my pelt," she whispered. Somehow, selkies are conduits of magic. She should have realised their furs did something special as well. Her mouth opened and closed, the words struggling to form in her mind, let alone be voiced. "You stole my pelt." The one in her hands crackled as she held it to her face, unable to stop the tears and burying them in the dried-out depths of the long dead selkie's skin.

"Darla. Please. I have a reason, a good reason."

Her shoulders heaved. "Magic has come back and you're wasting it getting *food*."

He took a step back, face going pale. "That's not… I'm not…" He balled his fists, claws retracting slowly. "The magic is helping to support the realm while Orla figures out a plan of attack, and then—"

Agony shot across Darla's side. She screamed, and flailed for whatever attacked her, overbalancing. Rory caught her before she fell down the marble steps of the dais and wrapped her close to his chest, the fur crushed between their rapidly beating hearts.

She lashed out, nails catching him on the cheek and raking across his left eye. He swore but did not let her go, setting her on her feet. "Why did you scream?"

Darla twisted in pain, scratching in his hard stomach, and he grunted but did not let her go. "Something's hurting you! What is it?"

"You!" Darla shouted. "Get away from me."

Rory let her go as if scalded, but stayed within striking distance. "Please, Darla, I want to help you."

Cold pain clenched like jaws around her stomach. The sight of him filled her with rocking nausea, bile tracing up her throat to mingle with the sickly sweet chocolate.

"Help!" Rhiannon sprinted into the throne room.

Rory stepped in front of Darla. "What is it?"

Darla hissed at his stupid bulky back blocking her view. "Rhiannon, are you alright?"

Panting, Rhiannon drew close, and all the hairs on the back of Darla's neck stood to painful, prickling attention.

A shred of grey-brown skin flapped in her fist. "Can't you feel it?" her friend asked her.

"It's damaged. Someone..." Her throat hurt trying to get the words free. She pushed past the pain. "It's torn." No. No!

Rory's breathing grew harsh. "I will fix this! Rhiannon, how long ago did this happen?" he demanded.

"Just now," the small fae said, her gaze darting between them. "Orla asked me to meet her there but when I got there, there was this, and... and the magic is gone again."

Without her fur sustaining this new surge of magic in the realm, it was going again. Wrapping her arms around her chest, Darla hugged the dead selkie's skin to herself. She couldn't touch the scrap of her own, in case she shifted into a seal. Or likely half a seal, or even just one flipper. There was barely enough in Rhiannon's hand to cover a finger.

"I'm going," Rory said, voice a low hiss like pressure escaping. "I'll get it back, Darla. I'm so sorry, I never meant for this to happen."

"No, you didn't." Bitter tears seeped out, scorching her cheeks. "You meant for me to never find out, you filthy thief."

Rory flinched as though her words whipped him. "I will retrieve your fur."

"I don't want you anywhere near it! I'll get it." Darla marched toward the doors.

Rory skidded alongside her. "Stop! Darla, whoever has it could get through all the best protections that Orla placed on it. They will have powerful gems, like rubies to burn or kyanite to attack your mind."

"I don't care, I'll bite them!"

"You don't know how to fight, please, stay back. I won't fail you, I swear."

"You already did." She shoved past him.

"Darla!" Rory sucked in a breath. "I'm calling in that favour."

CHAPTER 18

Rory

Their earlier bargain came into play, arresting her headlong dash and bringing her to an abrupt halt.

Rory ground his teeth together. She was dreadfully upset, skin sallow like she could collapse at any moment, face drawn with pain.

In Rhiannon's hands was the scrap of fur, Darla's fur, the fur he had captured and brought here and now it had been damaged. He had to hope it was only this small piece ripped off and not into more. His hands were still with purpose, his heart beating slowly. He had to fix this. What had broken through Orla and Kater's strongest protection wards? What had gotten past the guards? What could slice a selkie fur? All the answers pointed to the Cu Sidhe, and an attack force would be able to overwhelm and hurt Darla before they realised she was the victim here. They might even kill her, if they meant to take the fur to release the souls that composed it.

Darla's hatred of him burnt in her eyes as she struggled against the compulsion. "What are you doing?"

Rory lifted his chin. She might hate him for eternity, but at least she would be alive to do so. "Darla, you will go to your room and stay there, until either I return or three days hence." If he died, she would only be trapped for a short time, and people could bring her meals. Rory looked away from her seething hatred. "Rhiannon, please look after her."

"Yes, Rory," Rhiannon said, essaying a small curtsy.

"Don't you dare do this!" Darla screamed.

"I'm truly sorry." Rory paced out of the room, enduring each and every one of her curses and cries. He deserved them all and more.

Rory's steps quickened as he neared the tumbledown tower where the tether to the Worldheart waited. He had no weapon, but he wouldn't need one if he shifted. Claws and teeth were close combat, and he relished ripping the throat out of the one who had hurt Darla.

He had hurt Darla. Stealing her skin looked bad with that fucking pelt decorating the throne room. Why the hell hadn't he spotted what it was before? It was now impossible for her to believe that he did it to help her and the realm. Instead, it seemed as though he meant to sacrifice her life to sustain others'.

Did Orla know that pelt was from a selkie? What were Orla's true intentions toward Darla, and others like her?

There was a ruckus in the tether chamber, guards lying scattered. Rory headed there, a snarl rumbling in his throat. Orla's face was a rictus, teeth sharp as she snapped, "How did they get in?" to a guard.

The woman winced, holding her halberd with a shaking hand. "I don't know, ma'am, the team on guard has all been overwhelmed." She jerked her head toward the fallen fae, healers with green emeralds hurrying between them. "When they wake up, maybe they'll know?"

The queen spun away from the lackey and marched toward Kater. He was crouched near to a plinth underneath the thick glass where Rory had placed the bag containing the fur. It was empty.

"Well?" the queen demanded. She noticed Rory out of the corner of her eye and glared up at him as if this was his fault.

Rory squared up to her. He was done being manipulated by Orla. "What happened?"

Orla spat, "What do you think? Someone was able to spirit the fur away, just as we were finally getting ahead for once. It has to be the Cu Sidhe. They are the only ones powerful enough and with the gall to invade our lands." Claws pricked through her gloves, curved and shining with deadly intent.

Rory grabbed Orla's elbow. "Did you know that the pelt on the throne room is a selkie pelt?"

Kater reached to rip Rory off, but Orla raised her other hand, forestalling him. Her face drained of colour. "So, that's what it is?" She swallowed hard. "Rory, I swear I didn't know. It was our mother's, and likely she inherited it from her mother, and all the mothers before her. It's very old." Her gaze softened, searching Rory's eyes. "Is Darla upset?"

Rory dropped his hands to his sides. If Orla really had not known, then perhaps she hadn't been manipulating him to hurt Darla after all. Only to use her. "Of fucking course, she probably thinks we are going to feed her to the Worldheart. That might be what happened to previous selkies, why they felt they needed to hide." The air seemed sticky, his breathing shallow.

"I'm so sorry."

Rory kneaded his forehead roughly, welcoming the pain. "I need to get her skin back to her." Whatever happened after that would happen. Maybe Darla would stick around to listen and understand, or she wouldn't. Rory had played his hand poorly and he deserved Darla's scorn.

Orla nodded once. "It must be in Cu Sidhe territory or heading there. Go now and intercept it, I'll get Kade to meet you there. I'll watch over Darla and let you know if I am able to discover anything."

Rory balled his fists. ""I need all the gemstones we have." There was no other option. He would retrieve that pelt or die trying.

CHAPTER 19
Darla

"It's going to be alright," Rhiannon soothed.

Darla barely heard he. Her legs dragged her up to her room despite how she struggled against the compulsion. It was strong, and moving in any other direction caused intense anxiety to cramp her gut, existential dread piling on her.

The two walked along the corridor and finally into the room. Darla grabbed hold of the lintel but an invisible barrier prevented her torso from leaving, so she slammed the door shut. Screwing her eyes closed, she tried to breathe deeply and evenly. She had been tricked into entering the fae realm, where she was somehow a conduit of the magic the realm needed. Of course, they would have gone back and got her pelt. But Rory? *Rory?* Why had he toyed with her emotions like that?

"Because he can. He's immortal, and it's fun."

Darla's eyes snapped open. She didn't realise she had spoken out loud. "Pardon?"

Rhiannon sat in the centre of the bed, arms around her knees. "Ever seen a cat play with prey? They toy with it, let it think it has a chance of escape, watch it get nearly to safety, and then pounce." Her words were slow and measured, the cadence sending a chill down Darla's spine. "What are you saying?"

"That he played with you because it's his nature."

Darla's chest hurt. It hurt badly. These were the scars of the experience she wanted to have, and oh, how they hurt!

"I have an idea," Rhiannon whispered. "I think I can get you out of this room."

"You think?"

"Shh, just in case they are listening. Rory said you had to come here and then stay, but if someone else took you out, that's something you can't control."

Darla's heart fluttered. Could it really be that simple? Rhiannon went on, waving her arms in the air. "If we made it to the edge of the castle wards, there's an automatic spell negator there. That's to stop people from using magic against us, but I wonder if it works the other way." Rhiannon smoothed the palm-sized piece of fur in her hand. "It's so soft."

Darla shivered. She could not feel Rhiannon's slow strokes, but the sight of her sitting cross legged and pawing at the shreds of her fur made her stomach turn over. "I might. I don't know."

Rhiannon looked up. Her eyes were distant. "Hm."

"I want to track down where the pelt went. Can you take me where you found that? Then I'll look for clues and try to sense where it went from there." She glanced over at her friend. Rhiannon looked sad and awfully small in the middle of her bed.

Darla sat back on her heels. "How do you feel about that?" she asked quietly.

Rhiannon nodded slowly. "It will be well. I'll be going against my queen, but... if she's stealing selkie furs, I'm not sure I want her for my queen."

Being careful not to touch her fur, Darla hugged her tightly.

A FEW HOURS after night fell, Rhiannon opened the window. Taking Darla's hand, she pulled and heaved the bigger woman out onto the balcony. Sweat sprung out on every inch of Darla's skin, her teeth vibrating with an unpleasant energy and an iron taste in the back of her throat. She couldn't move her legs. Rhiannon helped her take stumbling steps, but the further she moved from the room, the worse she felt.

Darla dug her fingernails into her palms. They would not keep her here. He would not stop her! The very idea of his smirk fired her determination, but then she recalled the soft smiles that graced his face when she amused him. The upswell of feeling in her breast when she thought of his lips, swollen from kissing, lined with chocolate.

He toyed with her. Nausea flooded her mouth. He had kept her amused, and all it took was some kissing and chocolate. She shook her head at her own trusting naivety. *I'll take the lessons with me and never repeat that mistake again.*

Rhiannon whispered another charm which made Darla hover. Following like a piece of flotsam in an eddy, Darla could do nothing but squirm with discomfort as Rhiannon scrambled down the side of the balcony, down two floors, and then dropped into the manicured rose bushes lining the castle.

She flashed a small smile up to Darla. "So far so good." Trotting down the pathways, dark except for bright light from small lanterns lining the streets, Rhiannon led the way, and Darla could only follow, feeling sicker and sicker as they moved away from the castle.

"How long will this last?" Darla managed to grind out from between her teeth.

"We're getting close to leaving the town. Are you ready?"

"Yes. I'm ready."

Stepping out of the town, heat raced over her skin. She

winced, half afraid she would burst into flames, and Rhiannon's charm stopped. Darla landed on her feet, unharmed but wide-eyed, and the sick feeling had gone.

Rhiannon punched the air. "Yes! Ward and charm cancelling works on compulsions. I thought so."

"It's because I told you so." The low drawl came from the shadows outside the town walls. Lady Morag stepped into the lamp light, face set.

"Rhiannon?"

"I'm sorry, Darla, but this woman helped me once and I stupidly swore to a favour in the future. You are that favor." Misery etched Rhiannon's face. "I did say not to trust a Cat Sidhe."

Morag didn't worry about showing a flash of her teeth in her triumphant smile. "Now, we won't hurt you as long as you cooperate. You will come and see my mother, help bring her youth and life again. She's dying, you need to help."

Darla pulled her lips back from her teeth. "I have offered to help, but you all keep taking! Stealing from me, lying to me, trying to trick me! Enough. I won't be helping you."

Morag stalked closer. "This isn't cooperating, selkie."

Rhiannon looked between them. "You said you wouldn't hurt her, Lady Morag."

Morag ignored her, reaching for Darla's hand with claws extending, and Darla slapped them away. A sharp spike of pain shot across her fingers, and she cradled her wrist. Blood welled in shallow slashes.

Morag's face shuttered, as if preparing herself to attack again. She really was going to take what she wanted, and Darla refused to stand for it.

Turning on her heel, she ran away from the castle, away from Morag and Rhiannon. Away from Rory and Orla. How could she get home? Where was her pelt? Her chest tightened like as if clenched in the jaws of a predator, dragging her down into the depths.

Her skin prickled, and her steps slowed as if she'd floundered into a bog. Why? Why wasn't she running faster? She stopped and turned in place, facing Rhiannon and Morag again.

In between her and them stood a new figure, tall and wavering around the edges. A portal? Cracks and grunts echoed out from it, the shape mirroring small Rhiannon, whose eyes were wide and face ashen. Color appeared along its length like the shifting camouflage of a rock goby, and a second Rhiannon straightened up, grinning widely.

In its hand was the rest of Darla's pelt. It swung the golden brown skin around its shoulders like a shawl. "My master will be very, very pleased with you," the new Rhiannon said, her voice still high and happy.

Darla couldn't move, could hardly breathe. She was caught under the compulsion of her pelt.

The thing taking Rhiannon's shape smiled at the two Cat Sidhe. "Now, then. To dispose of the witnesses."

Darla couldn't even shut her eyes as Rhiannon screamed.

CHAPTER 20
Rory

Heading toward the Topaz Court, Cu Sidhe territory, Rory had to pace himself. Darla's pelt was in someone else's cruel claws, someone who had torn a piece off it to prove some kind of sick point. It was hard to feel righteous anger for the theft of an object that he himself had stolen in the first place, but he fanned the flames of it anyway. The disappearance of the fur had caused more problems than the loss of magic; it had highlighted to Darla that Rory was willing to lie to her. To protect her! He wanted to scream. She would kill herself willingly, trying to help everyone!

Passing the six-mile marker near the forest, he caught an odd scent. His hackles prickled. Blood and the sea.

Darla? Rory prepared to shift, the better to catch the scent on the air, when a stone thudded into the ground next to his hand.

Three shapes prowled from the trees. Short and stocky, their teeth protruded over their lips, clicking their long claws together as they paced toward him. Redcaps.

One threw another stone. Rory rolled, a hoot of laughter behind him, and a shattering crash shook his awareness, narrowing it to a black tunnel. Shit. A rock.

Red eyes glowing with grim intent surrounded him. Had there been only three? Now, there were six. Was that double vision, or reality? Sending his senses out, he could feel multiple living beings, but he was unable to count, groping for numbers with a loud ringing in his skull.

"Well, Rory." A gravelly voice as though filtered through sand and shale. Akir, the one who had led the trio of redcaps in the human realm. "I did say I'd skin you one day."

Swallowing, Rory's mouth filled with blood. He couldn't tell which way was up. Something grabbed his ankle, pulling; the side that hurt must have fallen against the ground. Now, fresh agony scraped down his back as he was dragged, bumping and scraping along.

Was this really it? Was he really about to die so close to home?

He would not die here. Rory's heart beat with a different tone. The cloying darkness had been pierced with a beam of light. Hope.

"There's only one fate for you now," Akir sneered. "You've run out of options!"

He always had options, but he couldn't see them through the daze, and time was rapidly running out. The redcaps were dragging him somewhere. If they made it into the forest, Rory knew he would never come out.

Instead he had an image of Darla, looking away from him into that tawny sunset.

I want to live. This thought was painful in its newness. It had once been a familiar refrain and had been lost for so long. It felt like the flutter of a bird's wing; fleeting and powerful. *I want to live!*

He could tear a hole in the Veil. He had the energy, reinvigorated by Darla's presence. He would end up who knew where, in any random century in the human world, but Orla would be able to find him if she applied resources to the task. There had been real shock on her face to learn that their mother's beloved shawl had once been a selkie's pelt. Orla wanted the best for the realm, but she wouldn't hurt Darla to do it.

Options, options. He could escape, relax into the embrace of death. He deserved worse, after what he had done to Darla.

Or.

He could fight on. Crunching a ball of concentrated magic in his fist, he shoved the energy from his hands to his emerald. Rory gasped as his vision cleared. Swiping the blood from his brow, he rolled away from the redcaps dragging his feet.

The redcaps hissed, raising rocks. "I knew we should have knocked his brains out!" Akir snapped.

There were three redcaps ahead and what felt like two behind. They were all in their true forms of small imps, the smell of old congealed blood flooding his senses. Rory shifted, claws sliding out, teeth bared.

Next to Akir stood a goblin with a knife. The blood dazzled Rory's senses, but that knife sang to him. Darla's blood. This was the bastard that had stabbed her at the beach. Rory roared, flinging himself forward and slamming into the redcap's chest. The goblin went down with a scream, and Rory clamped his jaws around his throat. One swift rend and his soul was gripped in Rory's jaws.

"Kill him!" Akir shrieked.

Rory turned to face the de-facto leader, the goblin's blood dripping down his chest and shoulders. Five against one were very bad odds, and he wanted to come out of this. He had to.

Akir lifted his knife as Rory leapt, but too slow. Rory seized his ear, the one Darla had bitten, and ripped it off. He quickly ended the screaming redcap, and the rest scattered.

Rory started running, but quickly the energy drained out of

him. He had healed most of his head injury, but there must have been lingering concussion. Limping back to the Cat Sidhe castle, Rory kept himself going with thoughts of Darla. Maybe they'd found the pelt under the sofa. Maybe the pelt would now be under triple guard, and Rory would insist that it was returned to her immediately. Then there would be some sort of indeterminate action on his part; of course, he should apologise, and somehow in his imaginings this led to her welcoming him with open arms.

Rory shook his head. He must have a concussion. Still, hope kept his paws padding along the road toward home, drawing him onward, pulling him toward her.

There was a commotion near the entrance to town with people swarming over a spot at the gates. A quick glance and Rory concluded that someone had met a terrible end, what with the blood splashes all the way up to waist level. The castle wards were damaged too, the magic humming out of tune, but he was too tired to do more than demand to be let through and stumble up to the castle.

He slumped against Orla's door, scratching weakly, and it opened to Kater's forbidding visage.

Orla peered around the bulk of a man. "Rory!" She tugged him in. "What happened? Why are you here?" Her eyes glittered with tears. *For him?*

Rory smirked, wincing when his face spasmed. *Probably not.* "Sorry I'm back, I suppose."

"Is that blood? Kater, go and get Rory an emerald." She gestured Rory toward the chair and handed him water, sloshing over the sides.

Rory drank with deep gulps, gasping. "Have you found the pelt?"

Orla's eyes widened. "No. What happened to you? What did you do?"

The glass nearly slipped out of Rory's fingers. He tightened his fist around it. "Some redcaps came out of their territory, close by. What happened here? The wards of the castle are damaged, I thought you would have felt that."

Orla shook her head, red curls bouncing. "Not with the magic as low as it is." There was a bitter twist to her lips. "It was so good to have it back to previous levels, when we had the… the pelt. But it has just illuminated to everyone how much trouble we are in. They are panicking, Rory."

Rory's jaw was so tight it clicked as he snarled, "The time for panic has passed. They knew about the problem. We've always told them!"

Orla put a hand on his arm. "Yes, Rory. But we also told them that we would lead them through it." Her eyes searched his. "Where is the pelt, Rory?"

The pelt. Not acknowledging the pelt's true owner. "Darla's pelt, you mean?" Rory straightened up, but pain shot across the back of his head. He slammed his free hand into the hardwood, relishing the bite of pain from his knuckles. "Damn it! Fuck!"

Orla's hand trembled, but she weathered his anger.

Rory curled his hand into a ball. "I'll get it back. I'll get it back." He closed his eyes, willing the magic of the land to rise up and bind him to his promise. "I swear I will get it back."

But nothing responded. They were just empty words, hollow promises. He would have to keep himself to his vow. Letting out a low breath, he tipped his head back. "How is our guest?"

Orla's face was still, but Kater slowly moved to stand a step in front of her. As if readying himself to defend her.

Rory frowned. "How is Darla? It's been, what, just one night? I didn't get too far. She's still in her rooms, yes? That was the stipulation of the compulsion I put on her."

Still no movement from Orla, and chills unfurled long claws into his stomach.

Her lips parted slowly, swimming in Rory's vision. "Darla

was somehow able to leave her rooms. She and Rhiannon... they are missing." She swallowed hard.

The glass smashed to the floor.

The Topaz Court, in the elemental domain of Earth

The cell door clanged shut, jerking Kade awake. How many fae days and nights had passed here in the dungeons of the Topaz Court? The iron around his wrists dragged his vitality out with every heartbeat and rendering his portal-making magic null.

A rattle on the bars meant to unsettle him merely hurt his sensitive hearing. A big hulking brute, Andre, drew a baton across the metal to make an ominous clang. Andre was the youngest brother of Shay, the Cu Sidhe king of the last court before the fall of the Worldheart river into the Otherworld. Teetering on the precipice over the mysterious land where the Cu Sidhe sent all human and fae souls on their way, the Topaz Court was an impenetrable fortress.

Until, that is, Kade had climbed it.

Andre rapped the bars with his weapon again. "Ready to talk, cat?"

Kade said nothing in return. There was nothing to say; he had been caught red handed climbing up the side of the castle within the bastion of the walls, and it was only a matter of time before Shay ordered him strung up and ripped his soul out to cast it over the roaring waterfall.

"I think he's weakening," a female voice said. A luscious, dangerous cadence, the voice which haunted Kade's dreams. He lifted his head from his meager bunk, too stunned to trust his ears.

Next to Andre stood a figure nearly as tall with half the shoulder-span of her brother. This was deceptive, however, for she was as strong as him; her strength was hidden in lithe muscle, her limbs as sculpted as if she had been carved from bronze. The Cu Sidhe princess Rosa's golden eyes raked over him, lip curled with distaste.

Kade sat up slowly, heart jumping in his throat and trying desperately not to show it. She was here? Why?

Rosa set her hand on the weapon dangling from her hip, her fingers lingering on the coils of a whip, curled like an obedient adder at her side. "Let me have the next hour with him, brother."

Andre snarled. "No, he was caught sneaking into your rooms, he clearly has designs on your life."

"All the more reason why I want to be the one asking the questions," Rosa returned, anger simmering under her tones. Kade shivered at the terrible promise in her voice. The iron shackles keeping his arms raised while he laid on the bunk rendered him helpless anyway, and they knew it.

Andre shoved off from the bars. "Alright. Have fun."

Kade counted the Cu Sidhe's steps as the heavy tread faded away. Yes, they faded correctly into the castle proper; he wasn't standing outside listening, he had left Rosa entirely alone with him. Not that she needed any help whatsoever; Rosa was as deadly as she was beautiful.

Rosa also kept her head cocked, breathing deeply and evenly as she too listened, every inch a calm, collected princess ready to extract her revenge one lash at a time. She stood still except for the movement of her chest, her breasts pushing against her tight armored corset, skin gleaming amber in the torchlight. All Kade could hear now were their exhalations echoing in the cell, and his own heartbeat, fast and getting faster with every passing second.

Enough time passed for Rosa to be satisfied her brother was gone, and she sprung into action unlocking the cell with shaking fingers, nearly dropping the key. The shining black rope of her hair slid over her shoulder as she stooped, panic now widening her eyes, and Kade's heart lurched with sorrow and shame. Once she flung open the door they could hide their true faces no longer; Rosa ran to his bedside and Kade arched his arms out for her.

"Kade, Kade," Rosa said, her tones torn between broken sobs and irate rebuke. "I knew you shouldn't have come, I told you!"

"I've risked it how many times now?" Kade offered her a small smile, a welcome patter in his chest seeing her eyes shining with the same fervent adoration he felt. "I had to see you, my love."

Rosa wrapped her strong arms around his naked torso, glaring at the iron chains. Kade pulled them away from her so they would never touch her perfect skin. Rosa was pure dedication, as loyal as the Cu Sidhe were reputed to be and passionate with it, oh so passionate. Kade sought her lips, Rosa bracing herself on his chest, and at last, Kade's thundering heartbeat was not alone. He lost himself in Rosa's sweet taste, stroking his tongue along her lips, swallowing the moans she made.

Rosa pulled back first, panting and skin shining with sweat as heat built between them. "We have to get you out of here."

"How will you do that?"

"I have the keys right here." She jingled them from her hip, a flash of silver and gemstones.

Kade jerked his wrists away from her reaching hands. "Won't suspicions fall on you if you're the last one to see me?"

Rosa scowled, pulling at the strands of her hair encased in her plait. Kade's heart melted afresh; nobody else got to see anything other than the polished and perfect Cu Sidhe princess except for him, and he usually coveted every second of it. Especially when she was thoroughly debauched, lips kissed to fullness, eyes glazed with the waves of pleasure he lavished upon her and lying spread eagle across whichever bed they had sneaked into.

But now his heart sat heavy in his chest, weightier than even iron. "I can't put you in peril."

"I'm in no danger," Rosa protested, and this forthright ire was also a side Kade loved, although perhaps not when he was trying to protect her. "My family won't hurt me," she insisted. "If anything, Shay will blame himself, and Andre will be too busy hunting you to ask any awkward questions. I can handle my brothers, Kade." She unlocked his shackles, rubbing his wrists.

"At last," he murmured in a hoarse whisper as he ran his hands over her armor, fingers finding the ties along her sides.

Rosa's lips locked to his, her kiss even more urgent as she murmured in his mouth, "Are you truly alright? Has anyone hurt you?"

"No, no," Kade promised, unwrapping her like a gift, slowly baring the princess to the cold air and his hot, searching hands. He stripped off her corset and unbound her breasts, taking her nipple into his mouth. Oh, her taste! He devoured her, every twitch and moan, his fingers delving deeper into her tight pants, searching out her folds. She gasped when his middle finger finally slid into her warmth, and he thrilled to find her slick for him.

"Mm," Kade murmured, lips arching up into a smile. "Seems I should add some chain play into our love making."

She shoved at his shoulder and Kade let himself fall back

prone on the bunk chuckling, but he couldn't laugh for long. His beautiful princess demanded his thorough and serious attention, and Kade intended to give her everything she desired and more.

She stripped off her pants, too eager to wait, and sat aside his hips yanking at his ties. Kade's cock sprung free, full and aching, and he guided her hands up to his shoulders so he could see her, all of her, his wild princess, queen of his heart. Rosa's expression softened, eyes glistening with love.

Still lost in her fathomless eyes, he eased her lower, arching up to slide his penis into her warm depths, and she tipped her head back with a feral cry of abandon. Kade loved every shade of Rosa, but he loved seeing her like this the most, unbound by clothes or rules, unfettered by the stupid war between their people, and defiant of the feud between their families. How could their love be an act of betrayal, when it felt so damn right?

AFTERWARDS, Rosa buckled up her corset. "I take your point about you escaping quite so soon after my visit," she said.

Kade kissed the back of her neck. "I have an idea. It's... a rather foolhardy one, though."

She turned her face to raise an eyebrow at him, a quirk of humor in her red lips as fire hot as any ruby. "Since when have any of your ideas not been foolhardy?"

Kade slapped a hand to his chest as if wounded, rewarded with Rosa's laugh. She always laughed quietly, as if afraid someone would overhear her and it was somehow a crime to be happy for even a short time, with the fae world fading around them. In Kade's ideal future, Rosa would be free to laugh long and loud, and especially at or with him.

He nudged her with his nose. "But seriously, this is a bit of an opportunity, if we can pitch it right."

Rosa wrapped an arm around his back. "Do tell, my darling."

Kade pressed her to his chest to feel the warmth of her breath and so she would hear his heart, beating strong and true for her. "The plan goes... a little something like this."

Thank you so much for reading! This is the second iteration of A Dram of Freshwater, where Darla takes her rightful place as the one who started it all. I hoped you enjoyed it! Reviews really help authors; I would be honoured if you would take the time to leave your thoughts for others.

Now, then... Where has Darla been taken, and by whom? That is Neri's question, and Darla's sister will begin her quest for answers in Book 1 of the Dark Tides series. Find out along with her in book one of the Dark Tides series!

THE SHADOW OF DEATH

A king with a broken crown.

Shay rules from the murky corners of the Topaz Court, a realm not many willingly travel to. It promises only one thing —Death. Duty eats away at the dark king, and as he escorts departed souls to the Otherworld, something—or someone—threatens to taint his kingdom and destroy the magic that sustains it.

A selkie searching for answers.

Seven years ago, Neri's sister disappeared on dry land over the sands. Neri has prepared every day since to follow after her and find what delays her sister's return to the waves.

Death hounds after the selkie. Shay shouldn't stand in its way; to upset the balance is to risk everything. Not even when her spirit stirs something inside him, something he thought long lost...

As the threat to magic grows, the selkie might be the key. Together, Shay and Neri traverse the realms to save their homes, their families, and perhaps even themselves. Will they succeed, even under the shadow of death?

Chocolate goodies

Author's note: I ran a competition on the Dark Book Boyfriends Facebook Group to suggest a chocolate dessert for Darla. I loved them all so much, I had to include them! See if you can find one to inspire you.

Thank you to all who participated!

@firekitty

INGUNN HELGEMO

Chocolate milkshake, but swap the milk with amarula, add whipped cream on top with chocolate sauce, chocolate sprinkles and chocolate shavings, serve it with warm sticky brownies and vanilla + chocolate ice cream covered in chocolate sauce and a few slices of banana on the side.

ANDRA PREWETT

Mississippi Mud Cake:

- Homemade Chocolate cake with pecans and coconut (both optional)
- After baked, top with marshmallows
- After melted, make homemade chocolate frosting with pecans (optional)

Sinfully delicious

CHEROKEE CRUM

I've personally made bourbon brownies!

LEIGHA MURPHY

My kids love my s'mores volcanos. I cut up puff pastry into equal squares. Stretch them out a bit. Add 3 chocolate pieces, 1 squished marshmallow then 1-2 more pieces of chocolate. Fold over. Crimp edges with a fork and cover with egg wash. When cooked I cut them open and add another marshmallow (well done) and drizzle Hershey's syrup on top.

SHANNON THIGPEN

My mom once made a grooms cake that was deviled food with brownie bits and chocolate chips in the mix. It had real fudge pieces in between the layers and the frosting with chocolate buttercream icing. It was topped with milk, dark and white chocolate shavings and the slices were served with chocolate dipping dots sprinkled on it.

JOANNIE SICO

Death by chocolate. It's a layer of brownies crumbled, a layer of chocolate pudding, a layer of cool whip, crushed skor bars(heath if you can't find skor) & then repeat those steps again. You may add coffee kahlua to the brownies but not if kids are going to have it.

DEBORAH POWERS

It doesn't get any more decadent than death by chocolate.

JOANNIE SICO

It's called Brownie Surprise. You have the brownie then you spread a layer of peanut butter(the surprise), & then once that is cold, a layer of chocolate frosting.

MICHELLE MENEZES

I only eat the desserts, I don't know what half the stuff is called. *(Author's note – I loved this so much, see if you can spot this in the novella!)*

Chocolate sponge base with cream frosting on top, then comes another sponge cake with nutella, then another layer of sponge cover it with chocolate frosting. Then add some crushed hazelnut, dark chocolate shavings and macarons on top.

BEKAH BERGE

Black Forest cake!!! Decadent dark chocolate chips with rich chocolate cake and yummy cherries in between layers. Then top it all off with a chocolate ganache glaze.

LYNDSEY HALL

A molten chocolate pudding, maybe with coconut cream on top

PENELOPE DAWN

Decadence to me means ALL the things! Brownies, cakes, tarts, a rich dark chocolate fountain with every imaginable fruit. Paired with champagne (or a glass of cold milk).

BECKY JAMES

Becky James is the author of The King's Swordsman series and coauthor of the Dark Tides series. Based in the UK, she has a deep love of the British countryside, canals, and all things fantasy; she devours anything that has magic, swords, good friends and good times.

Her series can be found wherever books are sold, and she is often floating around the socials!

www.beckyjamesauthor.co.uk

INTERVIEW WITH BECKY

HI BECKY! TELL US A BIT ABOUT YOURSELF.

I'm from Wales originally, then I moved to Scotland, now I'm trying out living in England. (I'll do Ireland one day to complete the set). I speak conversational Welsh, French and Japanese and eager to learn more languages. I am a massive extrovert, but nearly all my friends are introverts, so I know how not to energy vampire them. I will still talk your ear off though.

WHEN DID YOU KNOW YOU LOVED FANTASY?

I got into fantasy young, and I'm all for stories that use the settings / events to explore human nature and character-driven storylines. My first "grown up" fantasy writer was Eddings, and I love that balance of humour and heart.

I write NA sword and sorcery mashed with contemporary fantasy, about a cocky swordsman and his exasperated friends, and a fantasy romance series. I like noblebright, with world-building threaded throughout the plot, and anything unexpected. I love it when a story comes full circle and closes off nicely, ready for the next. My stories are heavily UK influenced, from the mythology and folklore to the settings (semi-rural British countryside and our canals feature a lot. Slightly obsessed with canals). I'll feature the dreaming spires of Oxford next to steel-crash impacted Sheffield, and there needs to be more about the laylines influencing Milton Keynes and the real story behind the Magic Roundabout in Swindon.

facebook.com/beckyjamesauthor

www.ingramcontent.com/pod-product-compliance
Lightning Source LLC
Chambersburg PA
CBHW030922060726
47591CB00005B/1637